PETER LIKINS

Coyote Speaks

CROSS COUNTRY RUN

PLikins@Arizona.edu
www.PeterLikins.com
Publisher: Darby Books, LLC

Copyright © 2015 by Darby Books

No part of this publication may be reproduced, stored in a retrieval system or transmitted, in any form or by any means, electronic, mechanical, photocopying, recording, or otherwise, without prior written permission from the publisher, except for the inclusion of brief quotations in a review.

Printed in the United States of America.

Cover and Interior Design: 1106 Design and Louis Maestas.

ISBN: 978-0-9970423-4-4 (print)
       978-0-9970423-9-9 (eBook)

Dedication

This book is dedicated to a school librarian
named Miss Billie Hunkin and a ninth-grade
English teacher named Miss Mabel Fitzgerald. They
were the inspiration for my early commitment to the writing
craft. I honor them by assigning their names to
similar characters invented for this novel.

Acknowledgments

A painting by Louis Maestas was the source of the portrait gracing our front and back covers and the cover page for Book I. I value his work and appreciate his permission for its use.

The image on the cover page of Book II was drawn from a photograph of my beautiful wife Patricia as a young woman.

Michele DeFilippo and her associates at 1106 Design provided critical assistance in the design and production of this book.

Coach James Li and members of his cross country team at the University of Arizona screened my manuscript to help me do justice to this remarkable sport.

Contents

Book I. Kit Coyote	1
Chapter 1. Running	3
Chapter 2. Harvest Games	31
Chapter 3. Gold	51
Chapter 4. Cross Country	79
Chapter 5. Wrestling	95
Chapter 6. Loving	101
Chapter 7. Killing	125
Chapter 8. The Hard Road Home	149
Book II. Another Perspective	171
Chapter 9. The Witness	173
Chapter 10. Sarah Whitewater	179
Chapter 11. Coming Together	213
Cast of Characters	249
About the Author	253

BOOK I

Kit Coyote

CHAPTER 1

Running

I have always been a runner. As far back as I can remember, I have always been a runner. Sometimes as a boy I was running away, running scared, but sometimes I was running just because it felt so fine, felt so clean and pure, felt so free.

I grew up in Southern Arizona on a chicken ranch just two miles south of the little town of Ajo (AH-ho), a few more miles north of what is now called the Tohono O'odham Reservation but was then called the Papago. Even before starting school I remember running on the open desert, maybe running away from The Old Man, the chicken rancher who, with his wife Molly, took in as many as ten foster children, myself included. He could never catch me on the run, but eventually hunger would

Coyote Speaks

drive me back to the ranch and Aunt Molly's irresistible cooking, knowing that her husband's angry but tolerable whippings were the price I must pay. It was The Old Man who first called me Kit Coyote, and to him that was a serious insult: The coyote in his mind were shadowy and elusive hobgoblins and a threat to his precious chickens. Coyote offspring, called kits (not pups), would grow to be troublesome varmints, and that's the way he saw me. His double-barreled shotgun was always close at hand, but only rarely did he hit a coyote — and even a wounded coyote can vanish from sight like a fleeting image in a desert mirage.

In my mind's eye I can see The Old Man even now: I see squinty eyes and a bulbous nose with red veins evident even across the room; I see very white skin where the sun had not yet done its work, the white skin of his protruding belly hanging over his sagging belt, his great paunch supported by skinny legs; I see the stubble of gray whiskers that always seemed just three days old, not yet a beard, stained by the tobacco juice that he unpredictably spat in the general direction of his handy coffee can. I see his big head and that leather thong around his skinny neck, knowing that a small brass key was knotted at the end, a key that was visible only when he was opening

4

Chapter 1: Running

his shirt to cool off at the water tank. Quick of hand but slow of foot, he was dangerous up close but easy to evade if I stayed alert to his presence, a skill I mastered better than others of the seven foster children then in his home. I learned much later that his name was Jake Durkin and his kinfolk were still back in Muleshoe, Texas, which Jake had fled after a barroom brawl left a man dead at Jake's hands. Jake and Molly never went back to visit kin; they never left the chickens to go anywhere beyond Ajo.

My memories of Molly Durkin (we called her Aunt Molly) are of a different kind: memories of the smell of her kitchen, smells that never left her presence except after services on Sunday when the scent of lilac lingered on her body; and a deep recollection of the sound of her voice, always comforting and reassuring. She was a buxom little woman, that I do recall, her brown hair with streaks of gray tied up in a perpetual bun and her faded dress nondescript, except again on Sundays, when her one black dress clung a bit too tightly to her mature body, stretching across the full breasts that she carried with modest pride. As Catty, the naughty girl, told the story, every Sunday Aunt Molly would drive the pickup to Ajo for services at the Southern Baptist Church, packing two or three of the foster girls in beside her, sharing in that truck her love of both God and the minister who brought his Word. Pastor Bob guided at least her spirit and maybe her heart, just as her husband guided and controlled her daily life. Apparently her pastor kept her straight on God's desires and only occasionally suppressed his own. Molly surrendered her heart to God and only occasionally surrendered to His minister, seeing no conflict between the two as long as she also met dutifully the needs of her husband. She saw it as her duty to be a buffer between her husband and the children in her home, and in subtle ways she kept him in check. But in the Arkansas country culture of her childhood the man of the house was not to be openly challenged.

I must admit that as foster children we were well fed. Although we routinely ate breakfast and lunch in the kitchen, taking turns at a small wooden table, the family dinner was always a major production, served by Aunt Molly and the girls at a dining room table that accommodated all nine of us, the seven kids on side benches and The Old Man and his wife enthroned on massive chairs at each end. Aunt Molly was limited by the workings of the ranch in the variety she could bring to her table. But she made the very best of what she had, buying such staples as flour, sugar, salt, pepper, and coffee at the Ajo markets but otherwise relying on what we could produce from

Chapter 1: Running

the chicken coops and the barren desert soil at the ranch. Aunt Molly was creative in the many ways she served the chickens and eggs that were the basic ingredients of her kitchen's offerings. Her dinners were augmented by vegetables from the carefully cultivated garden and fruit from our precious apple trees, which yielded not only fruit in season but the delicious stuff of Aunt Molly's apple pies and cobblers after preservation in her Mason jars. We enjoyed beautiful, golden ears of corn and red tomatoes harvested from our desert gardens and tolerated as well several varieties of squash, best appreciated by the kids as zucchini cake after the harvest season. Molly and the girls scraped and dried the corn, grinding the kernels into flour for the best corn bread I've ever tasted.

The Old Man tended his garden with more love than he ever showed to his foster children, who spread chicken-shit fertilizer, distributed scarce water, and hoed weeds under his watchful eye. He kept a switch in his hand for any laggard child who showed too little zeal in tilling that precious plot of land, just as he punished any perceived lack of enthusiasm in tending the hen house. Jake's tomatoes won first prize at the Pima County Fair in my second year at the ranch and his plump chickens won blue ribbons every year, so our enforced diligence had the effect

Coyote Speaks

The Old Man desired. Old Jake loved his vegetables, his chickens, his shotgun, and his old truck. We kids could only hope that he also loved his long-suffering wife, but we saw no evidence of that. Of one thing we were clear: The Old Man certainly didn't love us any more than an overseer would love his field hands.

In that sprawling old ranch house the Durkins kept five army cots in a basement room for foster girls and five army cots in a kind of slope-ceilinged attic or loft for foster boys, although those cots were never all occupied at the same time during my ten years there.

When I showed up on the ranch in August of 1946, there were three girls assigned to the basement cots: Mary (the oldest, maybe eight, and Molly's favorite helper), Catty (only seven but already dangerously unpredictable), and innocent Snow (maybe five).

Mary had a dark, round face and a body to match; she had a stolid way about her and showed no love for me, but she was never unkind. It seemed to me then that Mary never cried, no matter how badly she was hurting, but she didn't laugh much, either. She seemed happiest when she was talking to the baby chicks. Mary's parents were both dead, brought down by the three biggest evils on the reservation: alcohol, obesity, and diabetes. On the

Chapter 1: Running

county records she was Mary Smith, which always struck me as a pseudonym for nobody. Mary seemed resigned to her fate at the ranch and never complained.

Catty, in sharp contrast, was a lively and attractive little girl, showing off beautiful, long hair and a healthy, athletic body, her sparkling dark eyes set in a face the color of polished hickory. Catty was well aware of her charms, which she had already learned to use to her own advantage and to the detriment of any others who stood in her way. I never knew why she entered foster care at the age of five, but unkind rumors said her birth mother was in jail at the time and on the streets thereafter; no father was identified. Catty insisted that she was the sole survivor of the murder of her father, mother, and big brother in a bungled burglary of her family's big white house on the hill, but nobody believed her fantasies. I never did know Catty's last name, which she seemed to avoid using.

The older girls both kept me at a distance, but Snow became my special friend. A delicate child who might have been Chinese as well as Indian or Mexican in her heritage, she had been on the ranch less than one year when I arrived, so she was still making adjustments to that difficult environment. Catty told me (true or not) that Snow had been left on the hospital doorstep on her first

9

day of life, delivered clumsily in the neighborhood and abandoned immediately despite the rare snowfall that almost covered the ground. As soon as her hospital stay assured her survival, "Snow" was temporarily assigned to an orphanage, pending placement in a foster home or, even less likely, adoption. She must have been given a last name for the county records, but I never heard it mentioned. Foster families like the Durkins were reluctant to accept responsibility for children too young to do useful work, so Snow stayed in the orphanage until she was almost five, when the Durkins took her in and began training her to do her chores on the ranch. In her overcrowded and underfunded orphanage Snow had never felt the loving hands of a mother, but she knew from painful experience in that harsh environment that guiding hands could be rough, so she feared every touch but mine. Whenever she got scared, either on the ranch or in town, she reached for my hand, and I was proud to give her the sense of security that she so often needed. Snow saw me as her protector, and I accepted that responsibility seriously.

When I arrived at the ranch I was the youngest of four boys, the oldest boy a hotheaded, ten-year-old Mexican called Paco, the only non-Indian among the boys. Diego and Timmy were both seven, between Paco and me in

Chapter 1: Running

age. Paco's cot in the attic was close by the lone window, and mine was most removed and most oppressive on hot Arizona days, with the desert sun blazing through the roof. But it was worth the 110-degree heat to keep my distance from Paco.

He had been only five, orphaned by a sheriff's bullet that precipitated the death of his entire family, when Paco was dumped into the Pima County foster care system by authorities who had no good options. He had been traveling from his childhood home in the state of Guanajuato, Mexico, in the back of a panel truck with his family of six, all planning to work the rich agricultural fields of California's San Joaquin Valley as generations of his Sanchez family had done before him, but this time they ran afoul of the law. The Sanchez family was in a van that carried marijuana under the floorboards. The driver decided to run a blockade on Arizona Route 85, not expecting the deputy sheriff's bullet between his eyes and the crash that followed, killing everyone but Paco, who survived with no more than a wicked head wound that left him with a mean-looking scar, obliterating most of his right eyebrow.

Already angry when he was assigned to the Durkin ranch as a foster child, Paco's anger smoldered, fueling

Coyote Speaks

his appetite for trouble. It was Paco who first made the connection between the little brass key around The Old Man's neck and the brass padlock that secured the big red trunk in the garage, a building that was forbidden territory for all the kids and therefore often explored by the boys. Paco often boasted that someday he would wring The Old Man's scrawny neck, take the key, and raid the trunk, which he figured must be full of treasure. However, when Paco ran away four years after I arrived, The Old Man's authority was still unchallenged and he still wore that key. Years later I heard rumors that Paco was thriving in the cross-border drug trade, rumors that I found easy to believe. We all wondered if Paco would be coming back to collect that key.

Diego was a tough, hardy kid who had survived the violent death of his only parent with remarkable resilience, and already at seven years of age he was wise to the ways of the world. People called Diego handsome, a label they never applied to me, and I guess I could see why. He was a slender boy, but Diego was a healthy young animal, with a warm smile, white teeth, rich brown skin, and a shock of straight black hair that made him look taller than he was. Aunt Molly often said that Diego was a "cheeky boy," and I think I know what she meant by that.

Chapter 1: Running

One night at dinner, as we sat around that massive, old, oaken table, I remember Diego trying to cajole Aunt Molly into giving him the last beautifully browned chicken breast as she reached to bring it to her own plate.

"You don't need that breast," said the cheeky boy. "You already have plenty of breast."

Paco snorted and all six younger kids tried to stifle giggles, with varying success. I cast my eyes furtively toward The Old Man, fearing his reaction to Diego's oblique reference to his wife's ample breasts, but The Old Man didn't catch the joke and his only look was puzzlement at the suppressed giggling. Aunt Molly understood exactly what Diego was saying, however, and she couldn't resist a small smile as she surrendered the last chicken breast to Diego. He was cheeky for sure, but she liked him best among the four boys.

I lost track of Diego, but they say that he finished high school in Ajo as Diego Rivera and somehow found his way to Phoenix, a wilderness he was eager to conquer.

Timmy was quite another story, and not a happy one. I was always wary of Paco, running away from him whenever I could, and Diego generally tried to ignore my presence, but Timmy was my friend. I knew that Timmy would never hurt me, just as I knew that about Snow, but

Coyote Speaks

these two were the only people on that ranch that I fully trusted. Timmy didn't treat me like a nobody, as Diego did; Timmy showed me respect, and I gave it to him in return. He was a good-looking boy with striking eyes of a hazelnut color not often seen in Ajo in those days. He seemed to be most content when he was alone, seemingly lost in reverie.

Timmy took a lot of abuse at the ranch, mostly from The Old Man but also from Diego and Catty — especially from Catty, who teased him unmercifully. At thirteen Catty was ripe sexually before Timmy and I understood what was happening to her, but Diego (and apparently The Old Man) took notice immediately. It seemed to infuriate Catty that Timmy was indifferent to her budding sexuality, even when she staged a "chance" exposure of her new breasts to him in the bathroom shared by all the kids. (The Durkins had their own bathroom, never to be entered by any of the kids, unless Mary went in to clean the room.) Timmy was embarrassed and averted his eyes from Catty's nakedness, just as he would from Aunt Molly's. Catty found Timmy interesting and wanted him to look at what she had to offer, ignoring Diego's curiosity and mine.

Diego's teasing was incessant but always good-natured, directed at Timmy no more than at the rest of us,

Chapter 1: Running

but Catty had a mean streak in her. I let it roll off of me when she called me names (pipsqueak was her favorite, sometimes modified to pimpsqueak), but Timmy was cut to the core when she called him "queer." She tormented him for several years after the episode in the shower, often flaunting her sexuality in ways that she did not extend to Diego, trying to prove, I suppose, that she could change Timmy's natural inclinations.

Timmy's problems with other kids didn't end with our family. I didn't know it at the time, but for several years he was getting the same kind of bullying in school that Catty inflicted at home. I was struggling with my own problems making friends at school; I didn't pay much attention when Timmy tried to tell me his troubles. After it happened I wished I had been there for him. Maybe that would have made a difference.

We all relied on Aunt Molly for a sympathetic ear, but for Timmy that ear turned deaf when she caught him putting on nylon stockings and a garter belt that he had borrowed from her laundry bag. She was big on God's rules, and following what she and God saw as natural sexual roles was high on that list. Aunt Molly dragged poor Timmy to church that very day and exposed his behavior to Pastor Bob, who shared her shock and

Coyote Speaks

promised to pray for them both in a way that Timmy would not soon forget.

After services the following Sunday, Pastor Bob drove behind Molly's pickup in his battered Chevrolet, arriving at the ranch to the surprise of Molly's husband and the boys. (All three girls had crowded into the pickup to go to church that morning, but Catty had volunteered to join Pastor Bob for the ride home, easing the congestion in the pickup and providing Catty with an opportunity to demonstrate to Pastor Bob that at sixteen she was no longer a child.) When the dust in the yard settled, we were all instructed by Pastor Bob to gather together in a circle holding hands on the front porch, with Timmy standing in the center, obviously humiliated. We were told to repeat the Lord's Prayer aloud, with some mumbling coming from a puzzled but compliant Jake and the boys, setting the stage for Pastor Bob to pray in full voice for God's intervention in correcting Timmy's sexual deviancy (which was unknown and undefined for most of us in that circle). Raising his voice to a roar, Pastor Bob called upon Timmy to confess his sins and return to the arms of God, eliciting from Timmy only an anguished cry and urine running down his leg, staining his pants and extinguishing his pride. Timmy collapsed in a heap, and the circle broke

16

Chapter 1: Running

with embarrassment all around, but Pastor Bob quickly recovered his composure, declared the confrontation a success, and retreated to his Chevrolet.

After a troubled sleep that night, stumbling into her bathroom for her early morning ablutions, Molly was shocked at the horror scene in her bathtub: In a tub of bloody water, Timmy lay dead, a kitchen knife in his right hand, his left wrist still streaming red blood into the quiet water.

Molly's screams awakened the entire household, from the attic to the basement. All of us crowded into that small bathroom, a room I had never before entered, wanting to see but not wanting to see what Molly's stunned and tearful voice described.

Only at Timmy's funeral did I discover that his proper name was Timoteo Blanco.

Life was never the same for any of us after Timmy's death, but for Aunt Molly life as she knew it was over. Guilt and doubt destroyed her sense of self, breaking her spirit and sapping her strength, her body sagging as under a great load, just as the darkening bags of flesh under her eyes seemed to sag; even her breasts seemed deflated. For days and then weeks she rarely left her bed except when obliged to use the toilet, even then averting her eyes from

17

Coyote Speaks

that ill-fated bathtub, which she never touched again. She left the chores in the house, the washing, cleaning, and cooking, to Mary and Catty, but mostly Mary, who at seventeen was fully capable of running the household.

When Dr. Gutierrez was finally called from Ajo to the ranch, he found that Molly had irregular heartbeat that impaired her ability to circulate life-sustaining oxygen and triggered multiple ministrokes, recommending bed rest and constant attention. She was moved out of the big bed that she had shared with Jake for more than twenty years into a small bed newly situated in the living room, where she could be monitored constantly by Mary, whose duties grew with each passing month. Catty also had a new role to play, but the other three kids, Diego, Snow and I, were pretty much expected to do our chores and otherwise fend for ourselves, a freedom both Diego and I welcomed more than did little Snow, then fourteen but still lost in this dangerous world.

Pastor Bob came by to visit Molly after church services every Sunday for the first few months, sometimes taking Catty for a drive through the countryside after seeing Molly, but the visits to the ranch house soon ended, even though Catty's rides in that old Chevrolet continued.

Chapter 1: Running

Molly lived on as an invalid for several years and was still in that condition when I left the ranch.

The Old Man demanded that Catty take responsibility at sixteen for making his bed and maintaining his bedroom and bathroom, granting her full use of that bathroom for her personal needs, leaving Molly's care and most chores in the house to Mary. I was only fourteen at the time, but old enough to wonder what went on in that bedroom.

As a foster child on that ranch I knew I was expected to earn my keep, learning only much later that Pima County paid the Durkins for providing care for the foster children in addition to providing free lunches in school for wards of the county. In fact, Jake relied exclusively on child labor to run his very profitable chicken and egg business, paying no wages to the children, whose shoes and clothing were first acquired at Goodwill and then handed down from oldest to youngest with no shoes provided until required for kindergarten. Walking barefoot on the ranch's dirt and gravel paths roughened our soles and toughened our spirits; we laughed at the word "tenderfoot."

Coyote Speaks

This was the sordid reality, but as foster children we just did what we were told to do. Even a five-year-old boy can collect eggs in the early morning and shovel chicken shit to fertilize the garden in the evening, so those were the first jobs I can remember, even before I started kindergarten in Ajo. I envied the two oldest boys when they were called upon to man together the two-handled pump that drew from the well when still air left the windmill stalled. The pump included a three-foot, horizontal iron bar that pivoted about a support at its midpoint, with each end of the bar attached to a wooden handle in a kind of T, so each boy could place his two hands on his handle and pull it up and down, synchronized with the other boy. From the first day I saw the boys doing this work I wanted to be big enough and strong enough to take my place at that pump. When Paco left without warning in my fourth year at the ranch, I had my chance to prove myself. Soon I could match Diego as his partner at that pump, perhaps lacking his strength for the first fifty strokes but doing more than my share thereafter. Timmy was happy to yield this role to me; he said I needed the muscle more than he did.

The Old Man hated to see his foster kids leave the ranch to go off to school, and they had no birth certificate for me to verify my age (or my name), so they lied to keep me on

Chapter 1: Running

the ranch for another year's labors before I started school. When they first found me as a homeless child stealing eggs from their chicken coop, I told them my name was Joey and I was five years old on the fourth of July just past, but they called me Kit and called me four. I even showed them my brass belt buckle, which was shaped like a horseshoe and had the name JOEY on it, but still they called me Kit. I had almost forgotten, but I remember now that I told them exactly what my brother Jimmy had last said to me: "Run, Joey, hide. Go now!" They didn't want to hear any of it, and I began to wonder what was real and what was just imagined. I gradually buried my own memories and accepted their version of reality; Joey disappeared and I became Kit Coyote.

As inept as he was in caring for children, Jake was very skillful with his hammer and welding torch; he even crafted some fancy ironwork, welding to the tailgate of the pickup he used for deliveries an image of a basket containing eggs. Six bicycles kept in decent repair by The Old Man were housed with farm equipment in a rickety old shed on the ranch, bikes to be used by the other six kids to ride a couple of miles to and from school. When my time came to go to school, the Durkins were one bike short, so Paco was obliged to carry me on his handlebars

Coyote Speaks

all the way to school. He was by then eleven years old and still angry, resenting both his Indian foster-siblings and classmates and his Anglo foster parents, often cutting classes or skipping school entirely, leaving me walking home at first and then discovering that it was easier to run.

My oversized, hand-me-down Keds sneakers from Diego were too big for running, so on the way home I stashed them in my book bag and ran barefoot, as my Indian forebears did for many generations. In time, running to and from school became the best part of my day, the only time when I was truly free to think my own thoughts and dream my own dreams, none of which involved chickens.

The Durkins' ranch had a rather impressive entrance on Highway 85, with a grandiose name spelled out for all to see. Heavy wooden posts (like telephone poles) were planted on either side of the gravel driveway that led to the ranch house, with a massive beam spanning that drive, post to post, painted yellow to highlight the six-inch rusted iron letters shaped by The Old Man to spell the important name he had chosen for his property: RANCHO RIO SECO.

In truth there was no river on the ranch, only dry sand in a deep wash that carried flood waters after the summer monsoon rains. It wasn't much of a ranch either,

Chapter 1: Running

just a dozen acres with chickens and foster children. Most folks in town just called it "the chicken ranch," but for Jake Durkin the "Dry River Ranch" was the work of a lifetime, a private domain he had carved out of useless desert land far from every neighbor, a source of great pride.

On his ranch Jake had built a lucrative business, selling chickens and their eggs to markets and restaurants in town and even to individual families who stopped by, drawn by the carefully lettered signs Jake had posted to the left and right of his immense gateway: "Chickens and Eggs" on the left gatepost and "Pollos Y Huevos" on the right. He seemed to the good people of Ajo to be an upright citizen who shared his home generously with homeless children.

Jake and Molly had expected to raise a big family on that ranch, maybe ten kids as in Molly's Arkansas childhood home, or eight as in Jake's. After one stillborn child and a subsequent hysterectomy by a doctor Jake forever held accountable for his wife's barren womb, the expectation that a big family would work the growing ranch had to be abandoned. When Molly approached her disappointed husband about taking in foster children, he acquiesced for reasons quite apart from those that motivated his wife: Molly needed children to care for and Jake needed free labor for his ranch. They had both worked hard to build both

Coyote Speaks

the business and the ranch house they proudly occupied, and with this accommodation life seemed to be working out for both of them.

I'm told that when Jake and Molly staked out their homestead they lived first in a tent and then in a small house trailer while they built the first chicken house and its enclosed yard, giving priority to the need to establish a viable business before accommodating themselves.

That little house trailer was still on the property when I arrived, parked near the hen house on flat tires eaten by the desert sun, always locked but known to house Jake's welding equipment and other precious tools in addition to the original bed, on which Jake slept many Saturday nights.

One Sunday morning when Molly was at church I saw an old Buick, shiny under the dust of the ranch, drive right up to the trailer. The driver, a woman I later knew as Mrs. Hawkins, the proprietress of a string of cabins on the south side of town, opened the passenger door but did not get out of the car. A young Indian woman, a girl, really, quickly came out of the trailer and slid into the Buick, which made a trail of dust as it left the ranch. Apparently The Old Man was not always alone when he slept in the trailer on Saturday nights.

Chapter 1: Running

As resources permitted, Jake and Molly constructed, largely with their own hands, a ranch house that was quite substantial for its time and place.

Their tent house had been washed out by surprising monsoon floods in their second summer in Arizona, so they built the ranch house floor two feet off the ground, supported by 4"×4" posts lathered with creosote to discourage the abundant desert insects.

The eastern end of the house was dominated by a large kitchen augmented by a pantry and a wood room; the western end held the large master bedroom and full bathroom. The core of the ranch house was a generous living room with a large dinner table under high ceilings at the west end and a large desk at the other end under low ceilings supporting the loft, where the boys slept. By the desk on one side was the kitchen door, and on the other were two closet doors, one leading to a small sheet-metal-lined shower and the second to a tiny bathroom with toilet and wash basin (and no mirror that might encourage dawdling.) We kids showered weekly on staggered days, with each one of the seven kids assigned to the shower on a specific day of the week; a hose in the yard by the kitchen door was used for any special needs during the week between showers.

Coyote Speaks

A beautiful, oaken front door at the center of the north side of the house provided a fine entrance to the living room off a full veranda with split-rock steps shaped by talented stonemasons from Ajo, artisans who also constructed the fireplace that served both the living room and the master bedroom. But the front door was less often used than the back door leading to the kitchen through the service porch.

The kitchen door on the south side of the house opened to an enclosed service porch that accommodated outdoor gear and also provided access to the attic loft via one ladder and access to the basement by means of another. The outside door to the service porch was usually left open and latched to the side of the house, so a screen door was the primary entrance.

At the top of the first ladder there was no door, just passage to a floor that extended over the eastern half of the house with an open view of the dining room below, the edge of the loft defined by a railing about two feet high. Standing room was so limited that the four of us crawled into our army surplus cots every night in that slope-ceilinged loft. The lone window could be propped open to admit a little fresh air, but the loft was stifling on a hot afternoon.

Chapter 1: Running

The basement room was not entirely below ground level, so windows a foot high at the top of the interior walls provided access to sunlight on the east side of the room. These windows too could be propped open, providing some air but also inviting insects, lizards, and rainwater. The basement apparently accommodated five surplus army cots, but during my time there only three foster girls were with us. Boys were not permitted in the basement, so I never actually entered their room, but the girls called it their dungeon.

Despite its limitations, this was a fine house, really quite a grand house, and it should have been a good home for seven foster children with no other options. It was not a good home for any of us because The Old Man seemed to enjoy making life miserable for us all. Sometimes he pretended that he was tormenting us as a big joke, and sometimes he was reacting angrily to something we had done or failed to do. But it was impossible for any of us to know when he would strike out with the back of his hand, his wire-screen flyswatter, or any nearby stick, unless he pulled his belt from his pants for more serious and deliberate punishment. He never climbed the ladder to the loft to knock the boys around, but his occasional forays

27

Coyote Speaks

into the basement terrorized the girls, whose screams we could hear in our loft.

Jake's wife never screamed, but when she met the kids for breakfast in the morning she sometimes tried to hide the bruises inflicted during the night.

Jake Durkin was a violent and evil man, but he ruled his domain with an iron fist and there was no one there strong enough to challenge his authority.

When The Old Man wanted to "straighten out" one of his foster kids he usually held a family meeting, with all of us there to witness the punishment (although Aunt Molly often left the room). The victim was first humiliated by being stripped buck naked, then obliged to bend over, hands on knees, while The Old Man used his wire-screen flyswatter to administer swats on the bottom that stung badly and left temporary lattice-screen red images on tender skin but did no permanent harm except to the spirit. On rare occasions, when he was really angry, The Old Man used his belt, working himself into a frenzy as he bruised and lacerated the buttocks and upper thighs of his victims; Catty and Timmy triggered his anger most often. I saw Paco suffer this abuse twice; the second time, he ran for the border, barely fourteen. I felt the full force of The Old Man's belt only once.

Chapter 1: Running

I think that most kids in foster care "run away" for a few hours at least once, and when that happened at the Durkins' ranch the flyswatter treatment was usually administered as a lesson for all of us. On one occasion, however, when I was about ten, I made a serious attempt at escape and paid a heavier price.

One hot day in September I dawdled on my way home from school, playing with friends when I should have run home to do my chores, and I showed up just in time for dinner. Only after dinner was done and the dishes cleared from the table did The Old Man mention my tardiness, sending me out to the chicken coops to clean up as dusk was setting in. I took a shovel and an old lantern to light my way but dropped both when I rounded the henhouse corner to find a large bobcat facing me ominously. I ran for the house and told everyone what had happened to me.

To my surprise, The Old Man ordered me back to my henhouse chores, insisting that the bobcat was more afraid of me than I was of him. I wasn't convinced.

When I left the house again that evening it was to flee the ranch forever. I ran north to Ajo, hoping to hitch a ride to Phoenix and freedom. Instead I was rudely picked up by an Ajo policeman who knew me as "one of Jake's

Coyote Speaks

boys" and lifted me bodily into the back of his cruiser for the miserable ride back to the ranch.

Jake responded jovially to the cop's kidding remarks about his "runaway boy," insisting that I had been spooked by a bobcat, but when the policeman was gone the punishment began, my first and only encounter with The Old Man's belt, administered with anger driven by his embarrassment. As I "assumed the position" I cupped my testicles for protection and stoically accepted my beating, but my refusal to cry enraged him further. He kept hitting me with his belt until he was exhausted, leaving me bruised and lacerated, walking stiffly for days but proud of myself for taking all he could give.

I swore that the next time I ran away I would run far beyond Ajo and never come back.

CHAPTER 2

Harvest Games

Although I was excited to get off the ranch in my second year to go to school five days a week, I had a hard time finding my place among other kids, many of them already childhood friends from the nearby reservation, children laughing together over familiar games at recess, games I didn't know.

The laughter and teasing spilled over into the boys' bathroom, where all the boys in the elementary school shared a urinal trough, four toilet stalls, and six wash basins mounted below six mirrors, the only mirrors available to me. The ranch had a wall mirror only in the Durkins' bathroom, and the girls used hand mirrors. So in an elementary school bathroom mirror, I saw my

Coyote Speaks

image for the first time. I was shocked to find a brown boy with one pinkish-white cheek staring back at me. Was I part white in the sense that Snow was thought to be part Chinese? I agonized over this discovery for days before asking Aunt Molly my questions, eliciting from her an awkward silence followed by an indifferent response: "I'd guess you were born that way."

Even in the classroom I felt unwelcome, feeling ugly and awkward, too shy to speak unless called upon, and even then clumsy in my responses. For almost a month after school began I watched sadly from the sidelines at recess, alone and uninvited, and took my seat at the back of the room in class, trying to be invisible. I was rescued from this isolation by an unexpected opportunity.

The Harvest Games were a tradition in my community and at my school, a fall tradition that went back to a day when it was natural for an agrarian people to celebrate the end of the harvest season, mixing bacchanalia with demonstrations of skill in the arts and athletics. In my school, races were run all day Saturday on the high school track, grade by grade, with each winner qualifying for competition at the next higher grade level. We could compete at 50, 100, or 440 yards, all the way around that quarter-mile track.

Chapter 2: Harvest Games

At six years of age I was almost a year older than most of my kindergarten classmates and already a seasoned runner, so even running barefoot I easily won all three kindergarten races, probably earning more resentment from my classmates than the respect I craved. That respect began to grow when I won all three races at the first-grade level, too, and even at the second grade level won at 100 yards and 440 yards. I easily won the third-grade 440, despite having already run in three quarter-mile races that day, but I struggled to win the fourth-grade race at 440 yards, having already run hard for a full mile. This was the end of my winning races that day, but the community was buzzing with stories of the funny-looking little kindergarten kid called Kit Coyote who could run like his namesake. I was no longer alone and uninvited.

Mostly people talked with each other about my races and not with me, but I knew they were talking. Even the local weekly paper, the *Ajo Copper News*, reported on my exploits, surprising Aunt Molly and The Old Man, who were otherwise unaware. I listened to Molly chuckle as she read the paper aloud to her husband, and I heard enough to wish I could read it for myself. I didn't always like what she read, hearing myself described as "a freak of nature designed to run, with long limbs, a short torso

Coyote Speaks

dominated by a barrel chest, and the lean, hard look of a machine built of braided steel wire and spring steel."

"That's our Kit," she murmured. "That's our little Kit."

The Old Man's response to his wife was a snort. "Huh. I gotta admit he does run like a coyote. Wish he'd bring one of his kinfolk home with him so I could nail the varmint's hide to the shed."

I heard not one word of praise or even recognition from either of my foster parents, but all the other foster kids cheered as I beat their classmates in grades one, three, and four. Little Snow was most enthusiastic, telling her friends at school for the first time that I was her brother.

No kid wants to be portrayed as I was in that paper, but at least I wasn't being ignored by the whole world.

When the school principal, Dr. Eduardo Ramirez, called me into his office, I was apprehensive. In my anxiety I stopped at his open door when I realized that he was not alone. A tall, lean black man stood at the window, the blackest man I had ever seen, listening as my principal spoke urgently.

"You need to see this kid run," he was saying. "He's no more than six years old, but I believe that you can see his potential even now. You could develop him into an exceptional runner, which would be good for him and

Chapter 2: Harvest Games

good for your program." His voice trailed off when he realized that I was standing at his door.

Dr. Ramirez introduced me to his guest as his brother-in-law, Kenali Karangetti, whom he called "Coach K" (although he was at that time not yet a coach but merely a graduate student at the University of Arizona in Tucson.) Before that meeting was over, Coach K had invited me to come to Tucson with him to watch a cross country run, explaining that for shorter races we would have to wait for the beginning of track season. I didn't know how I would explain this trip to the Durkins back at the ranch, but even as a child I knew that I was being offered an opportunity that I could not let go by. Perhaps because Jake Durkin had a contract to supply the school cafeteria with eggs and chickens and was reluctant to deny the principal, or even his brother-in-law, I was permitted to leave the ranch as long as I doubled up on my chores when I returned to make up for lost time. I did so faithfully.

What I witnessed at that cross country meet changed my life forever. I discovered a full pack of serious runners in differently colored uniforms: men and women, not just kids like me, running just as hard as I ran, running through weariness to exhaustion, running like it mattered more than anything else in the world. I knew then that I had

35

Coyote Speaks

to earn the right to run with people like the cross country runners at the University of Arizona. Of course, I didn't know then that there was a world of runners beyond Tucson, runners I would join when my time came.

With a new sense of myself and the possibilities of the future, my attitude toward school changed dramatically. I began to realize that my inability to understand what was happening in the classroom came not from my stupidity but from my ignorance; many kindergarten classmates had come to school already knowing the alphabet, and some could even read many words, all reflecting learning experiences not available to me at the ranch. I began to see that I could apply the same focused effort to classroom learning that I had learned to apply to running. Catching up for me required months and sometimes years of hard work, but I finished fifth grade at the top of my class.

Coach K continued to be a quiet presence in my life, encouraging me both with his words and with new experiences that introduced me to the possibilities I could dream about and even work toward. He made sure that I had a proper pair of running shoes and made me understand that running to school was serious training for future races and working the pump at the ranch was a way to get stronger in every part of my body. I soon exhausted the opportunities

Chapter 2: Harvest Games

to run at my elementary school, and Coach K guided me into club sports and made arrangements for me to travel to regional events sponsored by the AAU, the Amateur Athletic Union. By the time I finished the fifth grade, the final grade offered at my little elementary school in Ajo, I was a serious runner, and by the time I finished eighth grade in 1956, ready for high school, I was a seasoned competitor, though not yet fifteen.

The difference between running and racing is profound, as I was slow to realize. In a race you have competitors, and for distance running that means that each runner is devising strategies for each race, altering his or her pace to match the circumstances of the moment. I knew how to run hard for a long time, but my normal behavior was to establish my pace and run constantly at that level, irrespective of the distance to be run or the challenges of my competitors, often starting slower than some runners and passing them later, but also running slower at the end of a race than some competitors, who managed to accelerate into a kick to finish the race ahead of me. Coach K tried to drive it into my head that I was not alone out there, that the idea was to get to the finish line ahead of every competitor, exhausting every fiber of my body just as I crossed the finish line, always first. Only after he was

37

satisfied that I had internalized this lesson did he explain the rules of scoring cross country team races, which may require the faster runner to shade his or her pace in order to keep a teammate in scoring position.

Along the way I realized that I would never be a sprinter: the longer the race the better my chances.

Something was happening to me beyond running and schoolwork during my years in Ajo's grade school: I was discovering in Coach K, his wife and two children what it meant to be a real family. Mama K treated all of her husband's runners warmly; but as the youngest of them all I felt especially welcomed in the Karangetti family, even as our lives intersected only occasionally during my overnight stays in Tucson for track meets on the following days. I couldn't tell Mama K then, but I hungered for her kind of family life, in stark contrast to the Durkins' foster family life on the chicken ranch.

The Old Man came home one day with a beautiful shepherd bitch in the back of his pickup truck — winnings he said from a poker game — intending to use that dog to ward off the coyote who threatened his chickens. He

Chapter 2: Harvest Games

said she was a German Shepherd and called her Queen, a fitting name for her in my mind even if she was less a purebred than he claimed. Instead of killing coyote she ran with them, even in heat, coming home with a bellyful of pups when no dogs were anywhere in the region. She was then driven to the back of the ranch to have her litter like a wild thing. Only one pup from that litter of five survived: a handsome coydog we called Solo, who soon got too big to be mistaken for a coyote. But Solo showed the characteristic gait of that remarkable animal, gliding smoothly over rough terrain in a seemingly effortless trot that swallowed the miles. I ran for hours with the dogs, first with Queen and then with Solo, who taught me, even as a little boy, to run while avoiding the thorns and sharp rocks that always threaten in the desert, even if I was tired. When Solo ran with me he always stayed just a few feet ahead of me, occasionally looking back over his shoulder and laughing (I swear he was laughing), urging me to try a little harder and run a little faster. Only when I fell to the ground exhausted did Solo relent, rushing back to me anxiously, licking my face and trying to revive me.

Running free in the semi-arid desert around Ajo carries dangers to every living thing. Thorns were an ever-present risk for Solo and me both, thorns that seemed to protect

39

Coyote Speaks

every desert plant, from the many varieties of cactus to the few native trees, from the prickly pear, the ocotillo and the cholla to the mesquite and the palo verde. On those rare occasions when a thorn penetrated Solo's padded paw beyond easy reach of his teeth he learned to lift that paw to me for extracting the painful needle, offering easy access for the fine-toothed comb that I always carried. Of course I needed that comb for my own encounters with Arizona desert plants, sometimes obliged to fend off Solo's attempt to pull my thorns with his front teeth so I could apply my more effective trick with my comb. Fortunately, Solo never suffered the potentially lethal strike of a rattlesnake or a Gila monster, nor did I.

On most mornings Solo would run with me as I left for school, always stopping at a large outcropping of rock just short of our nearest neighbor's drive, almost in town but never actually on Ajo's streets, stopping so I could put on those oversized Keds for school and Solo could remain behind and avoid the townspeople.

When I ran home after school I would always find him there, lying in the shade of that big rock formation. I'm sure he spent the intervening hours exploring the smells, sights, and sounds of the countryside, but he was always back at our customary meeting place when I arrived at

Chapter 2: Harvest Games

day's end, even if I had stayed an hour after school for some sport or delinquency.

Then one day Solo didn't rise from the shadow of the rock when I approached, and even when I called he was slow to appear, obviously limping, favoring his right hind leg. When I saw the buckshot wounds on his hindquarters I wanted to cry, first in sympathy with Solo and then in rage at the man or boy who had tried to kill my dog.

Walking was obviously painful for Solo but we made it back to the ranch and Mary helped me dig out the buckshot and dress his wounds, my brave dog whimpering quietly and flinching without showing his teeth or fighting off our efforts. Both Solo and I learned valuable lessons that miserable day, and I learned something about Mary, too: She treated Solo with more gentle and loving care than she ever showed to her foster siblings.

In school the next day I watched a boy holding his listeners in thrall with a far-fetched tale repeated from his father's boast at their dinner table: He had shot a wolf very close to town!

There were no wolves in the Ajo region in anyone's memory, so I had to conclude that the animal shot was my Solo, a combination of coyote and German Shepherd that could easily be mistaken for a wolf. I suddenly realized

Coyote Speaks

my sweet dog Solo, who would never hurt anyone, faced a danger I had never imagined.

Solo didn't forget that episode either, keeping his distance from strangers and showing his anxiety even at my side if a stranger carried a rifle or shotgun. This was a hard lesson, but I hoped that his resulting caution might keep him alive.

When Solo's wounds were healed, we returned to our familiar routine, running together most of the way to school and returning together at day's end. If neither chores nor homework were pressing in the evening, we would leave the road and take off into the desert or the dry sand of the big wash, running for the joy of it, running together as one.

The Southern Arizona landscape has a harsh beauty that has been enrapturing thoughtful people for centuries. The air is shockingly clear, so that distant mountains and even the moon and stars seem close enough to reach for. As the sun rises in the east, it casts shadows on the craggy mountains. The shifting light on the jagged rock seems alive as it crawls steadily across each mountain's face. Sunset brings these mountains to life again, and the beauty of the Arizona sunset is indescribable on special days when scattered clouds are illuminated with changing

Chapter 2: Harvest Games

colors as the sun goes down. Solo and I witnessed all of this together, sharing an aesthetic experience like none other.

I know in my heart that Solo felt the same reverence and awe in the presence of natural beauty that I felt myself. Anyone who imagines that only humans respond to beauty in their environment has never heard coyote bay at the moon. We humans alone have words to describe what our senses register in our brains, but in all humility we must acknowledge that our words are hopelessly inadequate to describe an Arizona sunset. Better that we sit in worshipful silence… or bay at the moon.

The terrain Solo and I covered when we left the road on our way home was rough, rocky, and hilly, creased by small ravines that fed into the big wash, becoming raging torrents during the summer monsoon season. Occasionally we would cross trails with small family packs of coyote, always disappearing like ghosts when they saw us. There were bobcat in the area, too, but they were very rarely seen, vanishing when they knew we were coming, almost always before we were aware of their presence. More dangerous were the family herds of javelina, the desert peccaries or misnamed "wild pigs" that roamed the area, omnivorous creatures with sharp tusks foraging for food (eating even the prickly pear cactus with their

Coyote Speaks

tough mouths) and protecting their young "reds," as their babies are called.

One late afternoon, as Solo and I ran along the edge of a small wash at the foot of a large hill, we surprised a javelina boar guarding his herd, and I recoiled as he charged. I stumbled backward, tripped over a rock, and fell into the wash, landing awkwardly at the bottom, twisting my knee violently, knocked unconscious by a protruding rock striking the back of my head. The rest of this story is pure surmise, but it must be true.

Solo distracted the boar, which never managed to reach my dog with his tusks, and the threat from the javelina passed. The old boar had no interest in attacking either of us if we stayed away from his family.

When Solo came to revive me at the bottom of the wash, I was initially unresponsive. Time passed as Solo paced nervously around my inanimate form and the desert sun left the sky, taking with it all the heat in the desiccated air. Desert nights can be freezing cold, even in Southern Arizona, and when Solo's big tongue on my face brought me to consciousness I was both extremely cold and acutely aware of the pain in my right knee. I managed to sit up but couldn't stand, both dizzy and unwilling to put pressure on my right leg. I laid down

Chapter 2: Harvest Games

again, dozing fitfully through the night with Solo's warmth curled around me.

Awakening at dawn I could see that my throbbing leg was swollen badly and Solo was nowhere to be seen.

Then I heard my dog, howling like a coyote from the top of the hill above me. He cried for what seemed like hours, but I know that Diego responded to his call and was led to me by Solo before the sun was high in the sky.

When on the previous evening I had failed to show up at the ranch after school, The Old Man told his wife and the kids that I was trying to run away and I wouldn't get far before hunger brought me back to the ranch, but by dawn the next day he decided to send out the boys to track me down. They fanned out across the desert in what would have been a vain search for me, hidden as I was in the wash, if Solo had not been crying for help at the top of the hill.

Diego and Timmy dragged me back to the road, ignoring my painful crying. Aunt Molly came to get me in the pickup, which The Old Man refused to do. She cleaned up my head wound and ignored the likely concussion, focusing on getting me back on my feet by binding my sprained and damaged knee with cold compresses. Aunt Molly's home remedies were all I needed then; both my

45

head and my knee eventually recovered, or so it seemed at the time.

This story would have ended differently if Solo had not warmed me and protected me through the night, calling my rescuers to my side when morning dawned.

I loved that dog with all my heart and soul, and Solo loved me back in that way, too. As a boy alone in the world, I loved Solo more deeply and more truly than I had ever loved anything or anyone.

Solo's mother, Queen, was a mature dog when she first came to the ranch and soon thereafter bore the litter that brought us Solo and four dead pups. She showed signs of arthritis before long, staying behind when I ran with Solo. The Old Man showed her more affection than he ever showed his wife, but he hated the very idea of her consorting with a male coyote and he certainly didn't want another litter of coydog pups. Jake decided to have her spayed "for her own good."

Doc Feldman, the old country vet who cared for the chickens' health, botched the spaying job, and Queen never came out of the heavy dose of anesthesia administered. Jake was so furious with the old vet that he knocked him to the ground, but he surely felt some guilt for calling for the unnecessary surgery in the first place.

Chapter 2: Harvest Games

Jake needed to vent his anger somehow, if only to deflect it from himself. In Jake's mind Queen had died because she gave birth to Solo, so Queen's pup became the focus of his misdirected anger.

The Old Man hated coyote and had always actively despised Solo, but after Queen died suddenly, Jake's antipathy turned to unreasoning hostility. When he looked at Solo he saw the coyote most responsible for Queen's early demise.

Taking care of Solo was my job (with Mary's help) and my pleasure, but late practices and track trips left less time for me with Solo than either of us wanted. Solo was drawn to the coyote females in heat and he sought their company, but the old male who led the pack made every effort to keep Solo at bay. My coydog was both bigger and stronger than any coyote, but it was not his nature to challenge in battle the leadership of the family pack; Solo was a lover, not a fighter. Probably he succeeded in seeding some promising offspring, but Solo was never accepted in the coyote family.

Nonetheless The Old Man decided that Solo was running with the coyote and a threat to his chickens, so he staked out a hiding place by the chicken coops and waited with his shotgun one night for the expected raid, a night

47

Coyote Speaks

when I was staying with Coach K in Tucson for a race the next day. The chickens were indeed a natural lure to the coyote, whose remarkable jumping ability made no chicken-wire enclosure high enough, and whose diligence as diggers challenged every effort to thwart their appetites. But that night the coyote pack never arrived, and Solo came home alone to find himself facing The Old Man with the shotgun. Unafraid, Solo trotted toward the master of the house and took the full force of the double-barreled buckshot in his face, collapsing at the feet of The Old Man. Solo died slowly, but he died dead.

I found Solo the next evening where he fell, left there at the chicken coop by The Old Man as proof of Solo's predatory intentions. Blind with anger, I raced around the ranch until I found The Old Man behind the ranch house with a shovel in his hand, unprepared for my assault but quick enough in his reflexes to deflect my blows with his shovel, knocking me to the ground with a stunning blow. I'm embarrassed to say I burst into tears and watched The Old Man's back as he walked away.

I staggered to my feet, found Mary and Diego to help me drag Solo to a proper resting place at the top of the hill where we had spent so many hours together, and buried him deep. Mary's stoic countenance rarely showed

48

Chapter 2: Harvest Games

emotion, but that night I saw the pain in her eyes and a single tear on her cheek. I was not alone in my grief. There was little to love in Mary's life, but she loved Solo and cared for him when I was away. As I shoveled the last clods of Arizona dirt onto his grave, Mary kneeled to the ground to murmur her farewell to her friend.

Then I ran and ran and ran, running with Solo's ghost; running south on Route 85 (snitching an apple and a handful of Hershey bars from an open market on the way) and then east on Route 86 through the Indian reservation, running through the night; holing up during the heat of the day at some isolated farm or gas station; foraging for food and water; wearing my new running shoes on hot pavement and running barefoot when the roads cooled; pausing halfway to Tucson in the little community of Sells, where a kind woman gave me fresh water and a sack of fried bread; and then running again through the night for I don't know how many nights; running all the way to Tucson, more than a hundred miles, running to Coach and Mama K.

CHAPTER 3

Gold

Mama K opened her front door one Sunday morning in August of 1956, intending to pick up her morning paper, and almost stumbled across a sprawling body too young to be a member of her husband's college track team. She fell to her knees, checking the pulse of the youngster with the expertise of the professional nurse she was, relieved to find that the pulse of the strange boy on her doorstep was slow but steady.

Mama K helped me to my feet, virtually carrying my fifteen-year-old, 110-pound, 5'2" body through her front door and into the nearest bedroom. (Mama K was a healthy, sturdy woman who outweighed me more than she might have wished.)

Coyote Speaks

Once I was laid out on Mama K's guest bed, I opened my eyes to thank her and saw the recognition in her warm brown eyes. She probably didn't know my name, but she knew me then as one of her husband's runners who occasionally spent the night with other young men in the small apartment over the garage. She asked me no questions beyond offering water (which I gratefully accepted) and food (I was famished, but too tired to eat). I slept my first deep and truly contented sleep in ten years, awakening late Sunday evening to familiar voices as Mama K tried to explain my presence to her puzzled husband.

I strained to capture every word when I heard Mama K say that she had already been in touch with the Pima County agency that sponsored the Durkins as foster parents, but as I listened I heard encouraging news. I discovered later that Mama K was "Nurse K" to her patients and some colleagues where she worked as Head Nurse in the Pediatric Ward of Pima County's Kino Hospital, so her call to that county agency was a Sunday afternoon conversation with her friend the director, who reluctantly agreed to my temporary stay. Mama K didn't yet know that my "temporary stay" would last for four years, or that she would become the most important mother figure in my life.

Chapter 3: Gold

When I reached out to Coach and Mama K, I was too young to comprehend what it meant for them to rescue me, what compassion and strength of character forged in their personal histories moved them to take such a troubled boy into their home and their hearts. What I know now of their backgrounds I learned mostly in our final dinner together after my high school graduation, an evening that I will remember for a lifetime.

Born as Teresa Marshela Ramirez in Nogales, Sonora, Mama K followed her brother Eduardo to the United States from Mexico on a student visa and proudly earned her nursing degree at the University of Arizona. She was an emergency room nurse when she first met Kenali. He was admitted unconscious with injuries sustained in an encounter with a drunken driver in a shiny new pickup truck that sped away after interrupting Kenali's late night training run. Teresa was leaning over his bed, hoping for signs of life, when his eyes opened and met hers, sealing between them an understanding that knows no words.

Kenali Karangetti was then a Sudanese student at the University of Arizona, where he had been recruited as a cross country runner on the advice of a Peace Corps volunteer, a former Arizona runner himself, who met Kenali in a Sudanese refugee camp in neighboring Kenya. Kenali

53

was developing into an excellent competitor when, in his senior year at Arizona, he was struck down by that errant truck. But by then he had been accepted for the graduate program that would lead him to a coaching career.

Teresa was an exciting young woman whose power was evident not only in her classic Mexican-Indian features but also in the graceful way she carried her sensual body, even in a nursing uniform. After that first bedside connection, Kenali was helpless in her presence, and even after the years of marriage and the two children that eventually followed, he was perpetually grateful for the love and support she gave him in full measure. When I arrived at their doorstep Teresa was a head nurse at the Pima County Hospital, and Kenali was an assistant track and cross country coach at the University of Arizona, raising their children while pursuing their modest dreams in family and professional life.

Mama K became the foundation on which I tried to build my life, a role she had also played for the lover who became her husband as he struggled to overcome the insecurities of a refugee seeking a new life in America.

Arrangements were made to enroll me in neighboring Sunnyside High School, which I entered after a brief recuperation under Mama K's supervision, nursing my

Chapter 3: Gold

blistered and bloody feet, sleeping in one of the three beds in the apartment over the garage, and eating ravenously at every opportunity. I was soon able to resume my practice of running to school and back, arriving early and returning after the workouts scheduled with the cross country team. I realized very quickly that even as a freshman I could hold my own with the best of the distance runners at Sunnyside, a school with a statewide reputation in wrestling and football, but not in all sports.

I found Sunnyside to be a more structured environment in which to develop my running skills, and it also gave me a new perspective on learning, which had always been for me a necessary chore and a challenge to be met grudgingly. I discovered at Sunnyside that learning could be great fun, especially in English Literature and History, where wonderful teachers found a way to connect the schoolwork with my struggle to understand myself and my life experience.

In some ways the school librarian, Miss Mildred (Billie) Hunkin, was even more important to me than my classroom teachers. Miss Hunkin was a skinny, white lady who often wore her eyeglasses perched on the tip of her nose, scaring me when we first met just by looking at me over those glasses. Only later did I realize that she was assessing

55

Coyote Speaks

my potential before she embraced the challenge I presented as a poorly educated little Indian boy. She accepted that challenge and never let go; she was there for me for all four years at Sunnyside, guiding my reading and testing my understanding of her assignments. She never stopped challenging me, pushing firmly but gently, always with at least a little smile, an engaging humor in her eyes that made me feel appreciated. My time with Miss Hunkin was precious to me then, but even more valuable in retrospect.

I found that I could identify with Victor Hugo's Jean Valjean in "Les Miserables," a victim of circumstances in his youth but ultimately a man of great achievement, despite repeated tragedy. I read under Miss Hunkin's direction several of Charles Dickens's novels, from "Oliver Twist" to "A Tale of Two Cities," seeing myself in every imaginative tale. She sent me to Jack London's books as well, so I could see Solo in heroic conflict. Yes, she directed me also to such contemporary books as "The Catcher in the Rye," but her clear goal was to give her young charge a foundation in the classics that she believed every child should know. I will always be grateful to Miss Hunkin.

When I entered Sunnyside High at fifteen my language was so rough and unstructured I was embarrassed to speak and ashamed of my writing. By the time I graduated,

56

Chapter 3: Gold

almost nineteen, I had confidence in my language abilities, probably more than was warranted, but at least I had a strong foundation on which to build. Of course all that reading under the tutelage of Miss Hunkin helped me to appreciate effective prose, but my skill in constructing language was due primarily to one of my English teachers, Miss Mabel Fitzgerald.

Miss Fitzgerald was a feisty, little, gray-haired white lady who had high expectations (and serious demands) for every student. She paid little attention to the vocabulary of grammar, so I never memorized terms like "present subjunctive," but Miss Fitzgerald insisted that all of her students write and speak in clear, coherent sentences constructed according to the formal logic of diagramming sentences. Every word in every sentence had a proper role to play and a clear relationship to other words in the sentence, as illustrated on the sentence diagram. Every modifier had to be clearly attached to the word or phrase being modified. Consistency of number and tense was absolutely essential; a plural subject with a singular verb jarred Miss Fitzgerald's sensibilities and she reacted with an elevated voice and fire in her eyes.

I knew I needed help with language, so I absorbed the lessons from Miss Fitzgerald as eagerly as a chick imprints

Coyote Speaks

the early lessons from its mother. I acquired the habit of diagramming sentences in my head whenever I would write and even when I was speaking seriously.

When I read American history I was puzzled to find the many millions of American Indians who first occupied this land so marginalized and stereotyped, leaving me with more questions than answers. In an environment at Sunnyside dominated by Hispanic students and Anglo teachers I tried to hold my tongue, conscious of the bloody conflicts between Indians and both Mexicans and Anglo-Americans, but the questions unexpressed then stayed with me for a lifetime.

Although I made a serious commitment to the Sunnyside track and cross country teams and over the next four years brought statewide recognition to those programs, I continued to see Coach K as my principal mentor in track. He guided my entry into the regional meets sponsored by the AAU, which was well organized for the age-group competition that augmented and reinforced my competition on the high school team.

Surprisingly, the most powerful impact of Sunnyside athletics on my development came in the sport of wrestling, a sport in which I had little interest while I was growing up in Ajo. Wrestling was ultimately critical to

Chapter 3: Gold

my life experience, but that was not at all apparent to me during my high school years.

Living with Coach K and Mama K during my four years at Sunnyside gave me the best possible support system, and I prospered both academically and athletically. But in retrospect I realized that I was still a troubled young man when I finished high school. Too often I was distracted by wild thoughts and strange sounds in my head, sensations that I could suppress only by pushing myself physically to the point of numb exhaustion. What was surely a liability in human terms turned out to be an asset for a developing athlete, however, as I pushed myself mercilessly and in the process acquired a physical stamina that seemed unnatural and even superhuman to some competitors.

I was rarely living alone in that apartment over the garage, as Coach K provided transitional living arrangements for newly recruited international runners in track and cross country programs at the University of Arizona and elsewhere, primarily African students who needed some time to get acclimated to America. Coach K had been a boy in the Southern reaches of Sudan, near the Kenya border, and he had great knowledge of that region and great compassion for the young people who suffered there with little hope for decent lives. Coach K returned to Africa every year, looking for students with running potential as candidates for scholarships in American colleges and universities, not only at the University of Arizona but in other programs where he had connections. I had the privilege of knowing a succession of these students as my roommates above the garage, young men whose life challenges more than matched my own, helping me see my personal situation in better perspective. Except during my self-imposed agony on the run to Tucson and a day or two foraging before I was assigned to the Durkins as a foster child, I had never been without food to eat and a safe place to sleep. Many of my new African friends had faced starvation and violent death, risking their lives for the opportunity to come to America, as Coach K had a generation earlier. I realized that I had no reason to feel sorry for myself and every reason to be grateful for my blessings.

Cross country running and wrestling might seem to be poles apart, but they have this in common: Both place a high priority on stamina and the ability to manage pain. The many differences are clear: The runner runs alone, while the wrestler needs contact with an opponent; cross

Chapter 3: Gold

country runs require exertion at a carefully controlled level over perhaps thirty minutes without interruption, while wrestlers function at the highest possible level of effort for three brief periods, each only two or three minutes in duration as altered by pins and overtime. It might seem that the most obvious difference is the impression that wrestling is a form of combat, requiring a psychological makeup contrasting with that of a runner.

Until I found myself at Sunnyside High School, I saw myself as a runner, not a fighter. With some discomfort, I realized that my first impulse when confronted with danger is to flee, not to fight. But Sunnyside is a school with a deeply embedded wrestling tradition, and even in routine gym classes every kid is screened as a possible wrestler. To my surprise, after a single encounter with the sport of wrestling in my freshman gym class at Sunnyside, I was drafted for the team by the wrestling coach.

The singular purpose of a wrestler in a match is to control his opponent; the most dramatic evidence of control is pinning the opponent's shoulders to the mat. It's not about fighting; it's about control, first of oneself and then of one's opponent. If a wrestler is fiercely determined not to be controlled by his opponent, and driven by primal forces to avoid being pinned, any wrestling coach will take

Coyote Speaks

notice. It's not just the ability to control one's opponent that matters; it's equally important to have a deep aversion to being controlled oneself, even if that avoidance is painful.

What the coach saw in me when I was introduced to wrestling in my gym class was my absolute refusal to be controlled by my opponent, calling upon unsuspected strength in my wiry body to overcome what might have seemed to be superior force.

I was persuaded to attend an early season workout with the wrestling team to be tested against experienced wrestlers. In practice after school that first day, I felt like a little boy tossed into a deep pool to learn how to swim. I was expected to keep up with well-conditioned wrestlers doing stretching and strength exercises unfamiliar to me as we "warmed up," and then I was paired up for wrestling drills with the best wrestler in my weight class, a senior named Miguel who showed me no mercy, taking me down at will with a wide variety of take-down moves I had never seen before. Miguel was a mature Filipino wrestler of nineteen at this low weight class, playing with me as a man plays with a boy. I felt foolish and wondered why they wanted me there.

Finally the coach called for actual two-minute matches, and again I faced Miguel, this time with the entire wrestling

Chapter 3: Gold

team watching, expecting their captain to pin my shoulders to the mat within thirty seconds. He took me down as before and turned my back to the mat, but I refused to be pinned. I went into what wrestlers call a high bridge, with only my toes and the back of my head touching the mat, my body rigid and unyielding in this painful position as Miguel tried with increasing frustration to force my shoulders to the mat for the pin. With less than a minute left in the match and his teammates laughing at him, Miguel flashed anger and moved too far toward my head, enabling me to spin around to my knees to face him, earning a point for escape in the process. The coach's whistle brought the match to an end, as the whole team applauded my surprise performance. I passed that test and joined the team.

After the first few painful weeks I found that I enjoyed the wrestling workouts in a deeply satisfying way, enjoyed the physicality of testing myself against other wrestlers, even when I took a beating from wrestlers who were more skilled and more experienced, but not more determined. Just as my troubled mind found relief in the exhaustion that comes with running very hard, I found peace of mind in relentless and exhausting combat on the wrestling mats.

To the surprise of my coaches, I found that I could sustain a very high level of strenuous effort without losing

strength or speed, dominating in the final period opponents who pushed me around at will in the first period.
Stamina is as great an asset for a wrestler as it is for a
cross country runner.

Wrestlers compete only in their own weight classes,
and I was very strong for my weight, thanks to Coach K's
insistence that I work hard on the upper body strength
track requires, beginning with the pump handles at the
chicken ranch. My arms and legs were unusually long for
my weight class, so I could throw in a "leg ride," grab an
ankle, or heel trip an opponent who thought he was beyond
reach. That "freak of nature designed to run" (quoting the
Ajo Copper News) was also designed to wrestle.

Despite all these advantages, I was unable to break
into the team's starting lineup as a freshman. I simply
didn't know enough about the technical aspects of the
sport to match the skills of the senior who starred in my
118-pound weight class, the boy named Miguel who had
introduced me to the sport on my first day. My opportunities for outside competition were limited to a few open
freestyle tournaments I entered after the end of the season.
Most of the progress I made that year I owed to Miguel,
who worked me over every day in practice. While it may
seem strange to people who don't have experience in this

Chapter 3: Gold

singular sport, I found the hours I spent in a hot, sweaty gym working out on the mats deeply satisfying, even if I was getting beat up pretty consistently by Miguel or pushing myself beyond pain to prepare for the competition that awaited me in future seasons.

Although I continued to see cross country as the sport that brought me to Sunnyside High, my reputation as a Sunnyside athlete rests on my ultimate success as a wrestler, a competitor for statewide honors on a team that always aspired to be first in the state of Arizona.

Wrestlers compete for three periods, starting the first period in a neutral position, both standing and facing each other. In the second and third periods, alternating, the wrestlers begin side-by-side on hands and knees, one in control on top by virtue of an arm extended around the opponent's waist. My skills were better suited to mat wrestling, whether on top or bottom, so I ended up too often giving up the first takedown in the first period, when both wrestlers began on their feet, and having to come from behind to win. Because my stamina was exceptional and my wrestling on the mat was far better than wrestling on my feet, I often won matches that got off to a bad start, winning either by accumulating points or by pinning my opponent.

Coyote Speaks

In my junior year I was very proud to earn a bronze medal for placing third in the state tournament, fueling my appetite for the gold medal that I was determined to win in my senior year.

When that time came, I entered the state championships undefeated and progressed to the finals without faltering. In the final match of my high school wrestling career, however, I encountered an opponent from Phoenix who adopted a strategy designed to exploit my vulnerability in the standing position that begins every match. I didn't know him then, but he knew me.

The Phoenix wrestler quickly earned two points for taking me to the mat, but rather than leave me on the mat where he knew I could do damage, the Phoenix wrestler let me up voluntarily, giving me one point. He repeated this pattern throughout the first two periods, leaving me frustrated and behind in points, four to eight.

As the final period began I was on the mat and in control, but I needed five points to win unless I managed to pin my opponent.

My long legs made me vulnerable on my feet, but they gave me a very good "leg-ride" on top. From this position I was able to execute what wrestlers call a guillotine, a

Chapter 3: Gold

very punishing hold that ultimately brought the Phoenix wrestler to his back for the pin.

When I claimed my gold medal atop the awards platform, with the Phoenix wrestler receiving the silver by my side, I realized that my opponent very nearly defeated me by wrestling strategically, adapting his strategy to my strengths and weaknesses, a lesson not soon to be forgotten, a lesson not limited to wrestling.

When I graduated from Sunnyside High in 1960 and went to college to run cross country, I thought I was leaving my wrestling competition behind me.

My performance as a miler and cross-country runner at Sunnyside High was the primary focus in my senior year, but by that time I was looking beyond the state of Arizona for competition in AAU regional meets. As a high school senior I was competing in the "under nineteen" age group, so I was running against some fine young college runners as well as high school runners in the western United States.

My success in San Diego at the Western Regional Championships qualified me to run in the national cross

Coyote Speaks

country championships for men under nineteen, but the expense was daunting. Coach and Mama K matched the proceeds of a fundraiser at Sunnyside High staged for my trip, and I was able to make the long, confusing bus journey to Bethlehem, Pennsylvania, where the men's and women's cross country championships were to be held that year on a beautiful course at Lehigh University. I had made the cut as an individual runner, an unheralded young man from Tucson, Arizona, far from home for the first time and very much alone.

I didn't know that I was going to win this race, but very quickly I reached that state of mind at which winning didn't matter; a state I thought of as "the zone," shutting out the other runners on the course and running instead on the open desert with my coydog Solo, or maybe now with the ghost of Solo, brought down by The Old Man's shotgun. As I ran harder I felt my body's pain but did not yield to its seductions; rising above pain, my mind on a higher plane, so remote from my body that my brain suppressed signals demanding relief while still sending commands to push harder.

The roar of the crowd brought me back to reality as I approached the finish line, well ahead of the pack but conscious of a single runner at my back, rapidly closing

Chapter 3: Gold

the gap. I could hear my challenger's footsteps and his hard breathing.

I had learned to run in the desert with Solo, conditioned to establish a punishing pace near the limits of my capacity and run at that speed for miles, slowing or accelerating as the terrain permitted. The concept of a "kick" to take down an opponent at the end of a race was introduced to me by Coach K and still not naturally internalized. But this day I heard Coach K challenging me to dig deeper to find the strength to kick into a new gear, accelerating to the finish line. I responded to the challenge, picking up the pace just as my opponent pulled even on the course, leaving him devastated by my surge, off stride and unable even to maintain his own fast pace, falling back to finish ten feet behind the winner, Kit Coyote.

I fell to kiss the ground but quickly jumped up to receive my challenger's embrace and the applause of the biggest crowd of cross country followers I had ever seen.

The AAU Cross Country Championship was recognized by the award of a gold ring that year, rather than a gold medal, surely only gold-plated but very real to me. It was a substantial ring with raised letters around the perimeter that identified the wearer as the AAU Cross Country Champion, the highest honor I had ever achieved.

69

Coyote Speaks

The ring fit my hand perfectly, but I had never worn a ring before, never owned a ring, and I couldn't get comfortable with this boastful hardware on my hand. In athletic competition over the years I had won many medals, all tucked away in a cigar box that I could look upon when I needed good memories, but I couldn't wear this ring any more than I could wear those medals around my neck. That ring became my most valuable possession, but it was destined to find its home in that cigar box when I got home.

Cross country races don't end when the first runner crosses the finish line. The winning team is not determined until the top five finishers on each team complete their runs, and the race is not over until every straggler finishes the course. Awards ceremonies follow and people linger afterward, savoring the feeling of achievement as they wind down.

As that long day came to a close, a group of yellow school buses lined up to carry the runners and coaches to their respective hotels, many of which were in nearby Allentown. My bus was full of animated runners, the nervous energy that preceded the run now drained from every athlete, displaced by noisy relief that the test was now over, win or lose. I found my seat at the very back

Chapter 3: Gold

of the bus, content to be alone with my thoughts, happy to be the winner in the biggest race of my life.

I reached back in memory to a time when I was always on the sidelines, watching classmates happily play their games, but now I could look upon my fellow runners from a more detached perspective with a new understanding. I knew finally that their laughter was not at my expense, that in fact my achievement was widely recognized and admired by other runners in that bus, but their fun stood apart from all that. I looked at individual runners and realized that I could not tell from their appearance or their demeanor who finished first and who finished last in the race. I noticed in particular a truly beautiful young woman sitting across the aisle just one row ahead of me but ignoring my effort to make eye contact, laughing with her friends with no attention to the winner in this race, enjoying the companionship of fellow runners in stiff competition.

What followed became a recurring nightmare, a confusing medley of memories so intertwined that I could not distinguish reality from frightening fantasy.

This much I would always remember clearly: A yellow school bus skittering across the pavement on its side, striking sparks as it spun lazily into the opposite lane, bursting into

Coyote Speaks

flames as it collided with an oncoming truck, the truck's side tanks of volatile fuel spewing across the wreckage. This much I would always remember: A lithe and lovely young woman, a fellow cross country runner whose accent betrayed her Jamaican heritage, ignoring my shy glances from the seat at the very back of the bus, suddenly propelled to the aisle at my feet by the gyrations of the careening school bus, whose driver swerved for reasons never to be known. I do remember landing on top of her in the aisle, so embarrassed that for a moment I didn't realize that she was bleeding profusely and not moving, her head smashed against the steel frame of the burning seats. My head was ringing, too, not from any blow but from the screaming in my ears, what seemed to be my mother's voice from childhood dominating other screams from the busload of cross country runners, some of them already enveloped in flames. Paralyzed by my own fear for just a moment, I realized as though from instinct or some buried memory that I must kick open the escape doors at the back of the bus; three hard kicks broke open the jammed doors and promised safety. Dragging with me the bleeding Jamaican girl, smoke curling from her hair, I climbed out of that burning bus, grateful to be among the few survivors, the others following me out that broken door.

Chapter 3: Gold

This much I would always remember when I tried to relive the experience, but there is much about that nightmare that I knew I would never understand. Why did I hear my mother's voice, her terrified screams, when she was surely not there, not there in any true memory? And why did I feel like a child, kicking at the back doors of that bus? Sometimes I believed there were two memories intertwined in my confused brain. At such times I put this entire set of painful images away in some dark recesses of my mind, to a place where I did not want to go.

The Jamaican girl was named Lani Beckman, running for an AAU club in the Philadelphia suburbs. In my mind at the time, however, she was just a stunningly attractive young woman, the kind of girl who had never given me the time of day, much less a date. I had admired her from afar, although sitting just one row apart on that bus, and then I became the man who saved her life.

The confusion following our escape from the burning bus was overwhelming, stunned survivors struggling with their own painful burns and bruises while grieving for their less fortunate teammates, feeling somehow guilty about leaving them behind in the fire. Groggy and incoherent but no longer unconscious, Lani was among the most seriously injured of the survivors, while I was

Coyote Speaks

least harmed. Ambulances were quick to arrive and we were all rushed to the Lehigh Valley Hospital and sorted out by the seriousness of our injuries. Lani was rushed to surgery, and I was treated and released.

The hospital lobby was soon crowded with a crush of concerned runners, coaches, reporters, and well-wishers, including the Lehigh president and the Bethlehem mayor, all anxious to thank me for a heroism that felt hollow to me. The host university, in its gratitude, offered to pay the airfare home that would spare me another long bus ride.

A reporter named Andrea Parker from *RUNNERS Journal* helped me to escape from the pressures of that hospital lobby and return to my hotel room, but then added to my discomfort by asking me very personal questions, trying I suppose to understand what made me who I am. Andrea's questions in my hotel room caught me off guard. I was unprepared for her probing into my private life, reluctant to open up old wounds.

"What's your secret?" she asked. "What makes you run the way you do?"

I felt foolish, fumbling for answers to her dumb questions, not knowing what to say. Why do I run? What kind of question is that?

Chapter 3: Gold

"Uh, I don't know. I've never thought about it. Why do I run? I guess I run because it makes me feel good."

"What do you mean, feel good?"

"Running makes me feel free."

"Free from what?"

"Free from everything. Running lets me get away from everything."

"Tell me more," she persisted. "What do you need to run away from?"

"The Old Man," I said. "And the chicken ranch. Most of all I needed to get away from myself."

"How can you say that, Kit? You just won a national championship! You saved lives! How can you be unhappy with yourself?"

"Today I won a big race. Yesterday I was a shrimp of an Indian kid on a chicken ranch in Arizona, a funny-looking, brown-skinned boy with no family, no name, and no hope. That's what I needed to get away from."

She caught me at a vulnerable time and was very persuasive; uncharacteristically, I spoke openly to her about painful life experiences that I did not normally share with anyone, talking into the late evening in my hotel room.

75

Coyote Speaks

I tried to sleep on the first leg of my flight home, flying to Atlanta for a brief layover before my long flight home to Tucson; I was both physically and emotionally exhausted, and I deliberately tried to sleep. My mind was racing, however, and whatever sleep I found came with nightmares that seemed like memories. I relived the accident again and again, hearing the screams, smelling the smoke, and feeling the heat of the fire. But I saw myself as a child in an old car, not a man in a school bus, and the screams came from my mother and not from fellow runners. I could not close my eyes without terrifying images crossing my mind as if engraved permanently on the retina of my eyes. I was reaching for my brother's hand, urging him to follow me through the gap behind the dislodged back seat of our father's old Ford. I was kicking open the trunk lid of that car from within, hearing my brother as I squeezed into open air, telling me to run from the car. In my delirious mind I ran away fast as I heard the car explode behind me. I ran and I never stopped running.

As my plane finally approached Tucson, I tried to get my head straight. I had won the race and "rescued the fair damsel in distress." I should be proud, I thought, walking tall. That's what Coach would expect of me, and that's

Chapter 3: Gold

what I must expect of myself. I put my troubled dreams behind me, burying painful memories.

Within a week of my return to Tucson, I received a Federal Express package from Jamaica, a small box containing a beautifully handwritten note of appreciation from Lani Beckman's mother, Lucinda, and a fine box containing a Rolex, the most magnificent gold watch I had ever seen, with an enclosed business card from Lani's father with the words "Thanks, Nigel Beckman" boldly scrawled on the back.

I had to read the note from Lani's mother a second time before I understood its underlying message. "Lani's father, her Beau, and I will always remember your courage in saving Lani's life. Beau's ring is by her bedside now as the burns on her hands heal, but the bond between them is not broken, all thanks to you." Lani's mother was telling me obliquely that Lani was engaged to be married to Beau in Jamaica. Lani's father's quick note was even more dismissive.

These expressions of appreciation from Lani's parents with their implicit signals struck me dumb, a response that seemed inexplicable to Mama K as she watched me open my FedEx package.

Coyote Speaks

I was, of course, grateful, as Mama K expected me to be, and appreciative of the protective love for their daughter reflected in their gifts. But at the same time I was struck by the clear signal they were sending me from a different world, from a place I could never hope to be. It had never occurred to me that a wealthy and cultured black family from Jamaica would frown upon their daughter consorting with a lowly and impoverished American Indian from the Arizona deserts, but I read that message clearly in their communications, both of them.

I labored for days before I sent my response to the Beckmans, trying to be appreciative and respectful without being presumptuous. I knew that I was expected to say goodbye to any fantasies I might have harbored about Lani Beckman and to be satisfied with the gold watch.

CHAPTER 4

Cross Country

After the excitement of my experience in Pennsylvania I had a hard time focusing on the imminent final exams I needed to complete for Sunnyside High School graduation, performing less well in my spring semester courses than I had expected of myself. Only after I had processed through the graduation ceremony did I allow myself to think about college, finally opening the letters of congratulations from college coaches who urged me to consider their programs. My AAU cross country victory had a greater impact on college recruiters than I had anticipated.

I had always assumed that I would stay with Coach K at Arizona, but my old coach and mentor urged me to consider all options. He assured me that he wanted me at Arizona, but as a very successful assistant cross country coach, he

Coyote Speaks

was being recruited for head coaching jobs elsewhere and could not promise me that he would stay in Tucson.

On the 3rd of July, the day before my nineteenth birthday, Mama K called me down to the main house from my garage apartment for a telephone call, as there was no phone above the garage. I picked up the phone not knowing who was calling, and was surprised to find Lehigh's Cross Country Coach David Chen on the line. We had met only briefly after my race at Lehigh, but Coach Chen had done his homework (apparently including a long conversation with Coach K) and was prepared to offer me a full scholarship to attend Lehigh in the fall, running cross country and also track in the 10k, pursuing a bachelor's degree in whatever field I felt best prepared to succeed. The Lehigh coach told me frankly that I was only marginally qualified for Lehigh academically so I would have to work hard to make it in that competitive environment. But if I was ready to commit myself academically my coach would make sure that I had every opportunity to earn my degree, with tutoring as needed and financial support assured for a full five years if that's what I required to graduate. Without hesitation and without even momentary consideration of other college offers that were coming my way as a

Chapter 4: Cross Country

result of my recent victory, I accepted Coach Chen's offer with thanks.

Coach K accepted my decision gracefully and in time shared my excitement in pursuing new dreams. He made sure that I learned all I could about Lehigh University and then joined Mama K in preparing me emotionally for independence as a young adult, sending me on my way to Pennsylvania with the blessings of the Karangetti family.

Only when I arrived in the Lehigh Valley did I begin to understand that Bethlehem was at that time (1960) a steel town, its people and its culture dominated by the powerful Bethlehem Steel Corporation. Despite what locals perceived as its ethnic diversity, there were no American Indians to be found, and few Mexicans. The Hispanics in the area were mostly Puerto Ricans. The "diversity" was essentially a diverse group of Europeans imported by Bethlehem Steel to work in the steel mill that dominated the town, people who saw themselves as very different from each other but all looked alike to me. The university students and faculty were almost all white and generally affluent by my standards. With a sinking feeling in my gut, I wondered if I had made a reckless and foolish decision. I was homesick even before I found my way to the little house near the campus where I would be living with other student athletes.

Coyote Speaks

The house I was assigned was in the middle of a block of older homes on a residential street squeezed between Lehigh University property to the south and Bethlehem Steel property to the north. In response to my timid knock at the designated address, the door flew open, and before me stood a young man who towered over me by more than a foot, his bushy red hair styled as an afro, a look I had associated with the newly labeled "Afro-Americans" in Tucson. This guy didn't look like anyone I had ever seen before, a man with freckles to match his red hair but with evident African forebears.

"Welcome, Kit," he boomed with a voice that matched his size. "You can call me Jeff." I later learned that his proper name was Thomas Bingham, but he was called "Jeff" in playful recognition of his descending from Thomas Jefferson, on the Sally Hemings branch of the family.

When I was ushered into that little house I was welcomed by three roommates, all athletes who would become friends and allies, each in his own way. I shared a room with a little white guy (about my size) from a coal mining town in western Pennsylvania, a returning Eastern Champion wrestler going into his junior year. His name was Damian O'Brian.

Chapter 4: Cross Country

In an adjoining room was a gigantic black kid from Philadelphia called Tenny, a football player almost as tall as Jeff but with a more powerful build. Like me, he was just beginning his freshman year. His roommate was Jeff, the man who met me at the door, a senior basketball player from Boston who measured 6'6" without the afro.

I could not have known it of my roommates at the time, but all four of us had entered Lehigh with liabilities to be overcome, all of us finally reaching the goals that brought us to the university.

Tenny (formally Tennyson Stark) had a rough start at Lehigh and very nearly flunked out at the end of his freshman year. He was a gifted athlete, excelling naturally in three sports in high school; a handsome and intelligent young man accustomed to success without effort in his Philadelphia ghetto high school environment. He loved to play and really didn't know how to work. His freshman year grades at Lehigh were disastrous.

Faced with the loss of his athletic scholarship and virtual expulsion at the end of his freshman year, Tenny was introduced by his faculty advisor to the university president, who was known to be a compassionate man. Appealing for help, Tenny promised the president that he

83

Coyote Speaks

would restore his scholarship eligibility by passing two summer session courses with B grades if he could only be granted the money required to pay tuition. Reminded that he would lose his NCAA eligibility for football if he received more money than had already been provided for the year, Tenny said he would gratefully accept these consequences if he could only stay in school and not go back to Philly, facing his mama in disgrace.

The president wrote a personal check for $600 to pay the tuition for two summer session courses, which Tenny passed with B grades.

Tenny watched his old teammates from the sidelines for three years as he learned how to do well academically, on schedule to graduate after his fifth year. The athletic director told him finally that he could restore his football eligibility for one year if he paid back the president, who had never expected to see his $600 again. The debt was paid and Tenny played football again in his fifth year at Lehigh, starting as a defensive end despite a broken hand suffered in preseason practice.

Tenny had a good year, but Lehigh was not scouted by professional football teams, so he had no realistic prospect to play at that level unless he excelled in the tryouts ("combines") held each spring by the professional leagues.

Chapter 4: Cross Country

Tenny surprised everyone but himself by demonstrating such athleticism that he was drafted and enjoyed a fine career in professional football. Tenny earned his success, but he needed a break when he was just eighteen.

Tenny had to dig himself out of a hole he created after he came to Lehigh. But Jeff had to overcome a disgrace that he brought upon himself in prep school, a prestigious institution near Boston that kicked him out for "scandalous behavior" that was never defined to Jeff's friends. With the doors closed to the Ivy universities he was expected to attend as a young man who excelled academically, athletically, and socially (until his fateful escapade), and moreover the son of a prominent Boston physician with Ivy credentials, Jeff came to a less judgmental Lehigh to redeem himself.

Jeff starred for four years on a basketball team that was very good by the standards of the league, excelled academically by every measure, and was elected president of a fraternity whose national leadership was appalled when they met him, not previously realizing his African forebears. Ultimately Jeff was accepted into Harvard Law, fully justifying Lehigh's admission decision.

Damian and I shared a room and ultimately much more.

The four of us got to be pretty tight, and when we later walked the streets of South Bethlehem together we

Coyote Speaks

must have appeared to be an unlikely bunch for Lehigh students. The two upperclassmen took seriously their responsibility to help the two newcomers get acclimated to Lehigh, a role formally assigned to them by the athletic director but not mentioned to Tenny and me at the time. Somehow the differences among us created a kind of solidarity, rather than isolation. Those guys helped me make Lehigh my home.

I soon realized that my life at Lehigh would be pretty much confined to academics and athletics, with very little time or opportunity for the social life that I expected to find in college. Lehigh was then an all-male school dominated by engineering students who let off steam in their fraternities, which were restricted to Christian Caucasians. There were pretty girls on campus for parties in the fraternity houses, and there were parties at nearby Moravian, Muhlenberg and Cedar Crest Colleges, where girls were enrolled, but this life was not accessible to me as a little Indian man from Arizona who deserved to be at Lehigh only because he could run. I learned very quickly to focus on studying for my courses and training for stiff competition in track and cross country, where I enjoyed the incomparable comradeship of teammates.

Chapter 4: Cross Country

I met with my academic advisor to select a major field and a course program, feeling both excited and somewhat intimidated. When the advisor understood my tentatively expressed interest in literature, he made an appointment for me with Professor Peter Beider, who welcomed my interest and calmed my fears, sharing stories of his sabbatical year with the Navajo in Arizona and the book he had written out of that experience, a novel based on a legendary Indian hero who had resisted the white man's invasion. I had the strange feeling that this white man was on the side of the Indians.

The cross country course was familiar to me from my one run there, when it was laid out for eight kilometers (a bit less than five miles), but it could be configured for races of varying distance. (Years later, the Lehigh campus was twice greatly enlarged to a magnificent 1,600 acres, accommodating an even more beautiful cross country course, but I found it impressive even in my time there. I spent countless hours on that course and it never lost its natural beauty.)

My time in winning the AAU national meet at 8k was 25:20, which was not record time for that course but notable for its era and sufficiently good to persuade

Coyote Speaks

Coach Chen to offer me a scholarship. When I joined the team in 1960 I had much to learn about race strategy and teamwork, and I knew that I had work to do in building my body to optimize performance. But I also knew I had the natural gifts that are needed for achievement at the highest level as a distance runner. I set high goals for myself both as a student and as a runner, and I went to work to achieve those goals.

I was a pretty good student at Sunnyside High in Tucson, finally earning Bs or better as a senior, but I was not well prepared for the rigors of a Lehigh University education.

Even with just twelve units in my first semester, I was overwhelmed by prodigious reading assignments and more complex ideas than I was accustomed to. Without the distractions of any real social life, however, I gradually mastered the essential skills in time management and learned to study in small groups with similarly stressed fellow students. I passed all my first-semester courses with Cs and gained confidence that I could do better. Tenny's freshman-year difficulty in maintaining athletic eligibility (and his scholarship) haunted me as I watched it unfold; I gradually established a cushion to protect myself from any disastrous grade that I might receive.

Chapter 4: Cross Country

The one area in which I was well prepared when I entered Lehigh was English Literature, and specifically American Literature, earning an A in the latter course and enjoying the experience greatly.

In American History, remembering the frustrations I felt in high school, I encountered the same dismissal of the millions of people who inhabited the Western Hemisphere before the arrival of European settlers. This time, however, I registered my objections to the class. I was, of course, the only Native American in my American History class, so initially I felt some dissonance in the response of my classmates. But my professor rescued me with high praise for speaking up and rewarded me with the responsibility for preparing and presenting a fifty-minute lecture on America's original people. When I delivered that talk toward the end of the semester and spoke candidly about the genocide that followed the European invasion, I got a standing ovation from my classmates and an A+ from my professor. That was my first time teaching in front of a classroom, and I found the experience exhilarating.

I learned a great deal from my classes in English, history, philosophy, psychology, and even geology and math, but even more important to me then was the confidence that came with that learning.

89

Coyote Speaks

Although I had won an AAU national cross country championship for runners eighteen and under, I was quickly humbled to discover how much tougher the races were against the older competitors I met in college, grown men with not only hard bodies but disciplined minds. I knew that I was not far from developing the necessary physical capabilities, but in my first few races at Lehigh I was repeatedly defeated psychologically.

When the fall cross country season gave way to track in the winter and spring I came to realize that my naturally developed aptitude for the rigors of a cross country course did not translate well to the oval track on level ground that I was confined to in track season, when I tried both the 10k and the 5k with only modest success. Clearly my event was the cross country run.

I placed poorly in some cross country races early in my first year at Lehigh, all races in which I might have placed in the top five if I had run a bit smarter on the hills or better paced myself. But by the end of my first season I was placing in the top three in most of my races. Coach Chen assured me that my physical skills would take me to victories as soon as I learned to race strategically.

My performance improved dramatically in my second year, when I became the top runner on my Lehigh

Chapter 4: Cross Country

cross country team and secured several first-place finishes. Lehigh's team qualified that year for the NCAA
Championships, to be held at the University of Oregon,
and in my own mind I was ready to leave my team behind
and run at the front of the pack to the finish line. Stamina
had always been a great strength for me, so I decided to
push hard from the starting gun, taking a lead and holding
it to the finish. I almost succeeded.

I took the lead as planned, but found a highly regarded
Oregon runner right behind me. I tried to lengthen my lead,
and together the two of us moved far ahead of the pack.
But the other runner stayed in my wake, letting me take
the brunt of the wind resistance. It was a blustery, windy
day in Oregon, with shifting winds seeming always to
be in the lead runner's face, an obstacle less significant to
the runner at my heels. I pressed on according to my plan
(not Coach Chen's plan) and the Oregon runner stayed
immediately behind me for the entire course until the finish
line was in sight, breaking away then to my right side,
nodding his thanks, and moving into a lead that he would
not relinquish, matching my kick with an acceleration of
his own. I learned a lesson but lost the race.

I vowed to run a smarter and more strategic race in
my junior year, following the guidance offered by Coach

Coyote Speaks

Chen and running more effectively with the team. That was my vow, but nature intervened.

During the summer after my sophomore year, I twisted my right knee playing Frisbee with Damian, and it locked up at a thirty-degree angle. The trainer discovered that he could unlock the knee by pulling the leg until the knee joint opened up sufficiently to free the obstruction in the joint; but the source of my problem had to be determined by an orthopedist. Imaging procedures revealed that knee pain and swelling I had been refusing to acknowledge for months had its origin in the deterioration of the meniscus cartilage in my right knee joint. The cartilage was almost gone, leaving my knee joint rotating with very little cushion, almost bone on bone. The knee injury suffered in my childhood fall into the desert wash probably started a gradual process of cartilage deterioration, resulting finally in fragments of cartilage getting caught in the joint, locking up the mechanism. The orthopedic surgeon told me that he could surgically trim the cartilage arthroscopically to take care of the lock-up phenomenon, but that wouldn't solve the problem. He said that I must stop pounding my knee joints on long runs, that my cross country days were over.

Chapter 4: Cross Country

I was devastated and deeply depressed. Running had been my life for many years, and it felt like life for me was over. I had to think hard about my situation and try to face reality.

Years of hard running destroyed my knees and cut short my career as a competitive runner, so my life was at a new turn, at an inflection point in the continuing twisting and turning of the arc of life. I knew there would be more unpredictable turns ahead, and I could not know at that stage of my life whether this blow would become for me the beginning of a prolonged descent or whether instead I could absorb this disappointment, as I had so many others, and find a path forward that didn't demand distance running.

It was running that brought me to the attention of Coach K, but the home I had made with the Karangettis for four years was not all about running. It is true that my tired legs took me from Ajo to Tucson, but that journey was more a reflection of my passion and determination than it was evidence of my capabilities as a runner. At twenty-one years of age I did realize that my sojourn from the chicken ranch to Lehigh University, from the Southern Arizona desert to the lush mountains of Pennsylvania, was

93

Coyote Speaks

not merely evidence of my ability to run. I had made the gigantic move from "running away" to "running to win." I had learned to compete, and that lesson could not be lost with the last race. I felt sure in my heart that there would be other challenges in life for me to face and overcome. I just didn't know then what these challenges would be.

CHAPTER 5

Wrestling

Damian O'Brian, a returning Eastern Champion wrestler when we first met, was a grad student and wrestling assistant two years later, when my cross country career came to a sudden end. He understood how devastated I was by my orthopedist's mandate that I give up my commitment to distance running. He knew that a big hole had opened up in my life, and he was determined to help me fill that void. Damian dragged me to Grace Hall, where the Lehigh intramural wrestling championships were being held, and urged me to enter the competition, which in that institution is very intense. Lehigh is always well populated by former high school wrestlers who can't quite make the Lehigh University varsity team, so intramural competition is fierce.

Coyote Speaks

With a total of only four years of wrestling experience and a gap of two years since my last time on the mats, I was not a very promising competitor, even in intramurals, but Damian knew that I was in superb condition physically and hungry for success. In that tournament I totally dominated three opponents, winning each match by either a fall (pin) or technical fall (outscoring by fifteen or more points) and earning gold.

Lehigh's famous wrestling coach, Billy Sheridan, took note. With Damian's help, Coach Sheridan drafted me for the wrestling team, slated to wrestle at 118 pounds, trying in my last two years at Lehigh to fill what Damian described as the void that had been created by his own graduation.

I lost my first three matches for Lehigh, but never by pin or technical fall, tightening the margin of the loss each time. I won my fourth match by coming from behind and dominating the third period. I finished the regular season without another loss until the Eastern Championships, where I lost in my second match by one point, losing in the process my eligibility for the NCAA Championship Tournament, where Damian had qualified as an All-American three times.

I was determined to do better in my senior year, entering the Eastern Championships with only two losses and

Chapter 5: Wrestling

hoping to qualify for the Nationals, which would require a gold or silver finish.

I was seeded fourth among the sixteen wrestlers in my weight class at the Easterns, but in my mind I was sure I could do better. Three hard-earned victories put me in the finals against the tournament's top seed, a nationally ranked wrestler from Cornell who was a bull of a man with seemingly impenetrable defenses and few offensive moves. There was no score in the first period, despite my aggressive attempts to take my opponent down. I started on the bottom in the second period and managed to escape and then take control early, staying in control with a leg ride and earning three points as well as a full minute of ride time as the period ended. In the third and final period I rode him hard for another minute, but in my effort to turn the Cornell wrestler over I moved too far forward to his head and lost control. I found myself reversed (for two points) and caught in a very dangerous pinning move called a cradle, on my back with my right knee pressed against my nose, held there by powerful arms hooked around my neck as well as my knee, good for three more points for my opponent even if the pin failed. Like a desperate animal in a life-threatening trap, I extended my

97

right leg and broke that powerful grip, and in the process cracked two of my own ribs. In the ensuing scramble I fought successfully for control (and two more points), oblivious to my damaged ribs. That made the score five to five, but as the match ended I earned one more point for registering riding time above the scoring threshold, winning that memorable match six to five.

This gold medal match was the toughest battle of my wrestling life, and it was also the last. Although qualified by my Eastern championship for participation in the NCAA Tournament, my two broken ribs robbed me of that opportunity. I didn't feel the pain until the match was over, but then it hurt just to breathe.

My wrestling days were over, just as my running days were over, but my graduation from Lehigh was on the near horizon, and a new life was awaiting me. I didn't exactly graduate with my class in the June ceremonies, needing to earn six more credits the following summer, but Coach Chen made good on his long-ago promise of scholarship support beyond my fourth year, and in September I was cleared for graduation with a BA in English. I accepted a graduate assistantship from Lehigh Athletics and enrolled after graduation in a master's degree program in education,

Chapter 5: Wrestling

hoping that after three years I would be able to join the ranks of the coaches who had been so central to my own development throughout my life.

CHAPTER 6

Loving

In the summer of 1965 Lani sent me a long letter from Jamaica, where she had lived in seclusion recovering from the physical and emotional trauma of the bus fire more than five years earlier. Although Lani's parents had written to me to express their gratitude soon after the accident, the tone of these messages had discouraged me from expecting any further communication. So I was surprised to learn that she was planning to visit her Aunt Sophia Longman near Philadelphia and was anxious to see me. I began to hope, perhaps to fantasize, that I would not face the future alone.

In Lani's letter, she exposed raw emotions, acknowledging the prolonged depression that had followed the bus fire and ensuing months in recovery, recognizing that over the years her psychic pain had gradually dominated

Coyote Speaks

her physical pain. She hoped that by returning to America and seeing me she could reconnect with the world she knew before the accident and regain some perspective. She also admitted some curiosity about "her hero," whom she remembered only as the guy from Arizona who had won the race, a man who saved her life only after she lost consciousness. (Apparently she never noticed that I was sitting right behind her on that bus). Was there a hint in her letter of fantasies parallel to mine?

I quickly responded to her letter, offering to meet her when she came to Pennsylvania and to help her in any way I could. Of course I did not betray the excitement in my heart as I allowed my imagination to leap far ahead of reality. I gave her phone numbers where she might reach me and waited eagerly for her call. For five weeks I heard nothing, and I gradually lost heart.

What made me think that this beautiful and talented young woman could ever care about the likes of me?

I tried to focus on my graduate studies and my job in the Athletic Department at Lehigh, discovering that my graduate coursework was easier for me than the more diverse undergraduate courses I had been obliged to take at Lehigh, and my duties in Athletics were more fun

Chapter 6: Loving

than work. I was just getting comfortable with my new responsibilities that fall when I got a phone call from Lani.

Her voice was so animated that I struggled to penetrate her Jamaican accent; only after I slowed her down did I realize that she was coming for the Christmas holidays to her aunt's home in Bryn Mawr, a suburb of Philadelphia, and wanted to meet me. Of course I eagerly agreed, my heart pumping hard.

The Christmas holidays were slow to come that year, but I stayed busy with the cross country and wrestling teams and with my own studies.

Through Lani's letters I learned her Aunt Sophia's address in Bryn Mawr. So I borrowed a Lehigh car and drove by to check it out, discovering an estate whose splendor I found daunting; no doubt reflecting not only her husband's position in commerce but also the affluence she shared with her brother, Lani's father. Aunt Sophia had two daughters somewhat younger than Lani, and these young women, Lani's cousins Amy and Natalie, were apparently the reason Lani's parents had approved of her visit to Pennsylvania. Obviously her parents were unaware of Lani's intention to see me, too, but her cousins were complicit in Lani's secret and romantic liaison with her erstwhile hero.

103

Coyote Speaks

I closed my eyes to the implied disapproval by Lani's parents and rushed to meet her in the lobby of the Hotel Bethlehem when she drove Amy's car from Bryn Mawr for our rendezvous. We met for an extravagant dinner at six, practically exhausting my carefully and painfully accumulated dollars, enjoying lobster with an unfamiliar wine followed by warm chocolate brownies topped with slivered almonds and drenched with the local Hershey's chocolate syrup. Bethlehem is known as "The Christmas City," and this was the holiday season, so we walked the historic streets of this beautiful old town for hours, pausing at the edge of an ancient cemetery, sitting close together on a massive old gravestone, heads almost touching in earnest conversation. Mostly I listened while Lani talked. The intimacy of her words surprised me.

"I've been dreaming, Kit, and you are in my dreams. I must get out of Jamaica and find my way to America for good, and you can help me. Do you want to help me?"

I had no words to respond, so I boldly kissed her on the lips, surprised by the warmth of her response, her hand reaching for mine, drawing it close to her breast. Eagerly I leaned in to put my free hand around her waist, pushing her right off the headstone, clumsily falling on top of her in the grass. I felt like a fool but soon joined

Chapter 6: Loving

in her laughter as we lay beside each other in the grass, awkwardly recovering to sit with our backs against the headstone, both trying to restore the mood.

"Lani, this is the second time I fell on top of you. The first time you were unconscious, lying under me in the aisle of that burning bus. That's when I fell in love with you."

I didn't mean to say it, but the words escaped my heart. I looked away from her in my embarrassment, greatly relieved when she kissed me gently on the cheek, reaching for my arm to help her to her feet.

"We have so little time," she said. "We have so little time."

At midnight Lani reluctantly began her drive back to Bryn Mawr.

During the fourteen days of her stay in Pennsylvania, Lani and I met just six times. But in my eyes that was more than enough time for me to fall truly in love, not just the flashing impulse in the burning bus, but truly in love. This was a new experience for me, and I reacted like a giddy teenager, blind to the realities of our fantasy world and oblivious to the consequences of our passion. For me, at least, this was passion, but it was at best adolescent passion on my part, even at twenty-four years of age. I had no experience with intimacy of any kind, not to mention sexual love. My only experience with sex had nothing to

Coyote Speaks

do with love, nothing more than one furtive union with a Sunnyside coed even more drunk than I was when we celebrated our high school graduation together. I was not eager to connect this mean experience with Lani, a woman I was sure I loved.

Although I could not keep my body from its yearnings, I kept my desires in check and did not risk any moves toward the bed that might seem to her premature. It never occurred to me in those exciting two weeks together that Lani might see our sudden romance through different and more experienced eyes, that she might have been there before.

I realized that the woman I embraced at the end of 1965 was not the same Lani Beckman that I pulled from that bus in the spring of 1960. She was no longer the strikingly beautiful, lean, and confident athlete that I first saw in that bus. Now she revealed a nervous anxiety and self-consciousness about the twenty pounds she had gained since her days of intense cross country training, fretting about the pink scar that creased her left eyebrow and disappeared under the hair that concealed her badly damaged ear. She was still beautiful, but she appeared to be insecure and vulnerable in some new way that went beyond her physical aspect. She was taller than I had remembered, but, of course, my memory was of a girl either seated on a bus or

106

Chapter 6: Loving

stretched out on an ambulance gurney. Lani towered over me by at least three inches, even without the high heels she insisted on wearing, perhaps trying to recreate that proud, standing-tall look she once projected as an athlete in running shoes. The changes that she surely deplored as flaws marring her perfection seemed to me only to make her more human (and more likely accessible to me). I didn't see these changes as diminishing her in my eyes, but I gradually realized that for Lani these were just the most visible of her increasingly overwhelming disabilities.

When Lani flew back to Jamaica after Christmas, we had a plan to make real our shared desire to spend our lives together. We would live apart, connected only by mail and telephone, until I completed my master's degree and had a real job. Then she would come to me in marriage, a legal union that would put her on the path to US citizenship, all this with or without her parents' permission. Lani and I made a pact and swore to keep it at all costs. We did keep that pact, but the costs were ultimately very high. We went ahead not only without her parents' permission, but without their knowledge. We paid a high price.

Coyote Speaks

I completed the coursework for my master's degree in the spring of 1966, at the same time laying the foundation for the thesis that I would write in the coming year. My project involved supervising Lehigh student athletes deployed to local high schools to motivate and guide high school athletes, work that gave me the opportunity to get to meet key people in several area high schools and gave them an opportunity to evaluate me.. As I had hoped, I was offered a position in one of these schools, Bethlehem Catholic High School, to work half-time as coach and half-time as English teacher, commencing formally in the fall after completion of my master's degree (but with the coaching informally effective immediately).

Even before that degree was awarded I plunged into my coaching duties, acting as assistant to both track and wrestling coaches at Becahi (as everyone called their school). I began teaching English only after completing that degree, fiercely proud to be entrusted with such a responsibility. I loved being a teacher, whether on the track, on the mats, or in the classroom.

Despite all my years as a competitive athlete, I discovered that the transition to coaching was very challenging. I had to learn to focus my energies and aspirations on other athletes, subordinating my own ego to theirs,

Chapter 6: Loving

understanding that a coach who remains focused on his own achievements cannot meet his obligations to his team.

As an assistant wrestling coach at Becahi, my duties included working with youngsters engaged in competitive wrestling before they entered high school. The lessons to be taught there are very basic but critical to success in wrestling (and perhaps in life):

1. If you get mad, you get beat.
2. If you try to hurt your opponent, you hurt yourself.

Especially for very young wrestlers who see themselves as fighters, these lessons are hard to learn, often requiring painful experience. Kids who lose their tempers lose control of both themselves and their opponents, almost always paying with embarrassing defeat. Wrestlers who focus on inflicting pain are losing sight of the goal of controlling the positions of both wrestlers, ultimately to pin the opponent, and any momentary loss of focus in a wrestling match can be fatal (figuratively speaking).

Of course it's true that the adrenaline that comes with anger (or fear) adds temporarily to strength and speed, but blind rage is self-destructive in wrestling, as in life. The coach's goal is to develop in his athletes a capacity for controlled aggression, so the surge in adrenaline and

Coyote Speaks

blood flow can be called upon at will. This concept is hard to teach and even harder to learn, but it is necessary for competitive success at the highest level.

If a wrestling coach does his job correctly, these lessons are so internalized that they remain embedded even after the last wrestling match is history.

I realized early in my life as a coach that my greatest joy came from teaching, not from the wrestling matches or the races that provided the test of learning. In both wrestling and track as opposed to football, basketball, and baseball, the coach's role is greatly diminished when the competition begins. The athlete is out there on his or her own.

Despite my dedication to my prospective job at Becahi, teaching English and teaching athletes, my dreams of my future with Lani were never far from my thoughts. My communications with Lani intensified with every step toward that day when we could come together. I had promise of a great job at Becahi, and my degree was almost in hand. We began to plan for our wedding, a civil union to follow my commencement in June of 1967, immediately after my graduation, which Lani would attend.

Lani had gained admission to Cedar Crest College in Allentown, Pennsylvania, a women's college sure to be

Chapter 6: Loving

approved by her protective parents, who would pay her tuition and living expenses. Lani's parents still did not know about Kit Coyote.

As I approached the two proudest days of my life, my master's degree award from Lehigh followed by marriage to Lani, I found myself dwelling with wonder on my attaining the unattainable; a homeless Indian boy earning a graduate degree from a prestigious university and claiming as his bride a classy woman of such grace and beauty. It all seemed unreal to me, far more than I deserved.

This commencement ceremony was solemn and serious for me, marking my entry into the world of adults as a working professional about to take a wife.

The very next day, Lani and I gathered at the Northampton County Courthouse for a civil marriage ceremony; Lani supported by her cousins Amy and Natalie, and my old friend Damian standing by my side. It was a simple wedding but the most exciting day of my life.

We had very little money that summer before my teaching job began in the fall, so our honeymoon was limited to a weekend at the Hotel Bethlehem. I ordered a bottle of champagne with dinner and took the bottle to our room, anticipating more pleasure together than dessert could offer.

Coyote Speaks

My most erotic fantasies had not prepared me for the indescribable thrill I experienced when Lani stepped nude into the shower I was taking before bed. I had only imagined the classic form of her body, her belly still firm if no longer hard, her small breasts beautifully shaped and begging to be caressed. I stiffened in anticipation of the consummation that awaited us, a young man and his bride.

Lani and I tumbled into bed still wet from the shower, frantic with desire. Only in retrospect did I realize that we were not well synchronized, that my complete satisfaction with our first sexual union came at her expense, my ejaculation coming too soon for her to share the orgasm. I didn't understand her disappointment until the early hours of the following morning.

My peaceful sleep escalated into wild dreams as dawn began to light the eastern sky. Lying on my back, I was mounted by a wild thing who looked like Lani, totally naked and sweating profusely, bouncing on my erection with animal energy, emitting subhuman sounds that rose to the level of screams as she reached her climax. Suddenly she rolled to her back with me still bound to her, accepting my pounding thrusts until we collapsed together, finally truly together. So this was how it was supposed to be. I knew I had a lot to learn about sex in love.

Chapter 6: Loving

The sun was well on the way to its zenith when I lazily left our wedding bed, wandering into the bathroom, leaving Lani still in the rumpled covers. I was puzzled to find on the bathroom counter a compact mirror still lightly dusted with grainy white powder, a safety razor blade and a short straw neatly resting by the mirror. I had no personal experience with recreational drugs at that time, but I knew I was looking at Lani's cocaine. Was this the source of Lani's aggressive sexual energy on our wedding night?

I realized too late for my reaction that Lani was standing naked right behind me in that bathroom, calmly inviting me to join her for a new high. "Try it," she purred, "and you'll like it as much as I do." Totally in Lani's thrall in that moment, I took the little straw and tried to sniff the cocaine residue on the mirror. There wasn't much there, but I got a small taste of Lani's pleasure. She followed with a fresh supply as we fell into bed again, this time making love more gently and more generously.

Although I surrendered everything to Lani for our honeymoon weekend, my well-developed instincts for self-preservation then took over, and I resolved never to use cocaine or any other hard drug again. Since childhood I had survived by being the master of myself, by exerting

113

Coyote Speaks

self-control to an extreme degree, even on the track or the wrestling mats. I could not knowingly accept the sacrifice of my self-control to drugs. I tried to keep up with Lani's drug use with alcohol, a more acceptable drug in my mind at the time, and also in the eyes of society; imagining that somehow this drug was different, this drug I could use without losing control. I was wrong, of course, but ignorance is the parent of drug addiction.

I tried to persuade myself that the shocking experience of my wedding night was a singularity, but I should have known even then that neither of us would be able to resist the twin seductions of sex and drugs. I thought I could protect her from the darkest side of cocaine if I avoided hard drugs myself and used alcohol moderately, preserving our sexual intimacies while going about our daily lives. I was very proud to be a teacher and coach at Becahi and believed that Lani would be similarly absorbed in her life as a student at Cedar Crest. I was ready to balance two roles in my life: a responsible, professional work life and a passionate love life at home, the latter fueled in no small part by cocaine and vodka. In the realization of all my dreams I was at the top of the mountain, but maintaining my balance was rapidly becoming very difficult.

Chapter 6: Loving

My job had many dimensions, and my dedication to my multiple teaching responsibilities required long hours. Classroom teaching occupied every morning, with coaching duties in afternoons, evenings, and weekends. The coaching work was a natural extension of my experience at Lehigh, but teaching English was a new and exciting adventure.

I taught two English classes every morning and staffed a study hall, which gave both the teacher and his students time to catch up a bit. Teaching English language skills was a challenge for me; my small elective course on Twentieth Century American Literature was both a challenge and a joy. I had read Hemingway, Steinbeck, and Faulkner at Lehigh, but seeing these authors through the eyes of my young students was a revelation. Faulkner's "As I Lay Dying" introduced these young readers to more literary imagination than they had ever experienced.

I found that the practice of diagramming sentences had fallen out of favor in academic circles, but I so valued the lessons I had learned from Miss Fitzgerald at Sunnyside High that I emulated her in my teaching, with a heavy emphasis on sentence structure as modeled by sentence diagrams. This was unfamiliar territory for my students, and not every kid wanted to accept analytical structure

Coyote Speaks

for language, but those who "got it" would have it with them for a lifetime.

My coaching experience in that first year at Becahi was also very gratifying. I didn't have the team leadership responsibilities of a head coach in either sport, so I was free to develop personal relationships with individual student athletes on the track and wrestling teams; helping them to work through internal conflicts and develop the self-discipline required for athletic success. I felt that I was teaching the techniques of both sports effectively, but my most important role was in the character development of these boys as they became men.

In the spring of my first year at Becahi I was elected "Teacher of the Year," an honor that meant as much to me as any gold medal I had earned in sports. I was very proud and deeply contented in my role as a teacher, both in the classroom and beyond.

Lani's experience at Cedar Crest College was less fulfilling for her, supporting the old adage that what you get out of college depends on what you put into it. She often skipped classes and missed deadlines in her first semester there, her grades in January reflecting her poor performance. At the end of her first full year at Cedar Crest, she was not invited to return.

Chapter 6: Loving

I was so absorbed in my own work that I was slow to realize that Lani had never had any intention of taking seriously her courses at Cedar Crest, which was for her no more than a ruse to keep her parents at bay. She never told her father that she was married or that she had dropped out (or flunked out) of college. He sent her a check to pay tuition for her second year at Cedar Crest, money that fed her growing appetites.

For Lani, however, my dedication to work seemed only an excuse for avoiding her and her problems. I gradually came to understand that her drug use was symptomatic of deeper psychological problems. She was high at times with no drugs to explain her mania and depressed for longer periods than a drug rebound would explain. When I suggested that she see a psychiatrist, she exploded with anger, insisting that her problems were not her fault (and were perhaps mine).

I tried hard to persuade Lani to take charge of her life and give up cocaine, but I finally realized that she was hopelessly addicted to her drug of choice. Meanwhile, my alcohol abuse was rapidly approaching that state as well. Our marriage rested on this shaky foundation from the day we wed. I always felt that sex with Lani was both thrilling and satisfying, but she wanted to mix sex with drugs, going to a place where I could not or would not follow.

Lani was abjectly sorry each time she came down from her cocaine highs, with remorse that consumed her (and exhausted her husband) until she countered her depression with more cocaine; progressing in the course of that first summer from snorting the drug to smoking crack. I tried with vodka to show her that I was anxious to join in her oblivion, hoping that she would switch to alcohol. But she used the vodka only as a sedative to temper her extreme cocaine-induced highs and then used more cocaine for a hit to shock her out of the resulting alcoholic depression. Managed in this way, her use of alcohol and cocaine escalated rapidly as the months of our marriage wore on.

Of course we quarreled about her increasing drug use, and my drinking hard with her on many nights just compounded the problem. We were losing touch with one another, sacrificing the precious intimacies that first bound us together. Drugs no longer enhanced sex; drugs replaced sex.

Lani and I also quarreled about money incessantly during our first summer together, as I was not yet receiving a paycheck and she spent the generous allowance

Chapter 6: Loving

provided by her daddy so recklessly that the rent for our tiny apartment was often delinquent.

One day, I wanted to show the cross country team the gold ring I had won in the AAU Cross Country Championships. But when I opened the cigar box in which it was always stored with my gold watch and other medals, I found it missing. When I realized that the watch I had received from Lani's father was also missing, I was devastated. Lani denied taking them, but I was angered by her denial, knowing that she had stolen my most precious possessions in order to fuel her appetites, crossing a line, going to a place from which she never returned.

Just before school started for both of us that first fall, she announced unexpectedly that she was taking a quick trip home to Jamaica that would resolve our money problems. Over my protest she flew home, returning four days later bursting with excitement and suddenly flush with American money.

Lani received a visit the very next day from a Jamaican man she introduced as her cousin Benny, although he seemed to me to lack the regal qualities that I associated with the Beckman family. Benny delivered a large, empty suitcase identical to the one Lani brought back from Jamaica (complete with her initials) and surreptitiously

Coyote Speaks

exchanged it for her now presumably empty case (although I noted the switch).

Lani's visits to Jamaica and Benny's subsequent exchanges occurred four more times that first year, over the Thanksgiving, Christmas, and Easter vacations, and again a few days before our first wedding anniversary in June; on each occasion stealing precious holiday time from her new husband while accommodating the expectations of her father, who still didn't know that she was married in America. Lani reacted with explosive anger when I intimated that she must be smuggling drugs, so I foolishly buried my fears. I was sure that Lani's drug abuse was somehow my fault, that I hadn't met her needs and had driven her to seek familiar relief in cocaine. Even in her darkest days I felt unworthy of her love, afraid I would lose her and still willing to risk everything to keep our marriage together. I knew I was being a fool, but a fool in love.

Lani was expected by her family to have Thanksgiving dinner in 1968 with Aunt Sophia and her daughters (Sophia's husband in Europe for weeks at a time), and I had hoped for an invitation to join her. I was looking for ways to begin some kind of relationship with Lani's family, hoping ultimately for help in restoring her health, but I

Chapter 6: Loving

was not invited. She went to Bryn Mawr alone, driving the sporty little red MG roadster that her father's money had provided, getting her head straight two days before her visit and apparently staying clean while with her aunt's family. Again I had Thanksgiving dinner alone.

Lani came home from Bryn Mawr in a relatively calm frame of mind, so we entered the hectic month of December with new optimism, tempered by the realization that I was committed to weekend wrestling tournaments that would take me away from her. That optimism quickly faded.

I came home late from a Saturday wrestling tournament the week before Christmas, anxious to give Lani a report on my team's victory, and found her raging at my absence in her time of need. She slapped me hard (for the first time) and told me that she was leaving me, slamming the door on her way to her car in the driveway, surprised to find me close behind her. I jumped into the passenger seat as she started the engine of her open MG, hanging on as she accelerated out the driveway, both of us shouting at each other without seeing the big Cadillac bearing down upon us in the street. With no seatbelts secured, we both suffered concussions, but Lani was on the impact side and took the brunt of the collision. The Cadillac driver was angry but unhurt.

Coyote Speaks

Police arriving at the scene soon concluded that Lani was driving recklessly while drug impaired, fully responsible for the accident, my complicity in her guilt not recognized by them but more than evident to me.

Lani called Amy from the hospital, and this time Amy's loyalty to Lani could not overcome her sense of responsibility to the family. She called her mom, who called her brother, Lani's father. The very next day both of Lani's parents, Nigel and Lucinda Beckman, showed up in her hospital room, arriving at a time when I was sitting glumly by her bedside, wearing tired sweatpants and a faded Becahi sweatshirt, unkempt and unshaven. This was not the way I had hoped to meet my wife's mother and father.

Lani's father was one of those tall, handsome, older men who dominate an entire room just by their regal entrance. His silver hair highlighted his tanned and ruddy face, two shades lighter in color than the polished mahogany on the yacht that I assumed he would have docked back in Kingston Harbor. Every word he spoke had the quality of command.

Lani's mother, in sharp contrast, was such a diminutive presence, and so meek in her demeanor, that she seemed not really to be there in that room at all. She had the yellow-brown skin of a Caribbean woman forever shielded from the sun. She spoke not even one word, not to me,

Chapter 6: Loving

and not to her daughter. This woman who had written to me such a beautifully personal note of appreciation when I saved her daughter's life was now silent.

Lani's parents ignored my presence in her room until I introduced myself as the cross country runner who had pulled their daughter from that burning bus more than seven years ago. They acknowledged my presence briefly, then turned back to Lani, dismissing me abruptly. I tried to insert myself between Lani's bed and her parents, insisting in a firm voice that Lani and I were then married, but her father put his hand on my shoulder to move me aside and otherwise ignored me. Before that day was over, Lani's parents had arranged for her immediate transfer to "a fine hospital in Kingston, back home" as her father said, overriding not only my objections, but also the pending legal charges against Lani for driving impaired. I protested as her husband, a marriage her father said would soon be dissolved, if not annulled. I felt helpless and did nothing to stop them, losing the love of my life without a struggle. Again, as with Jake Durkin, I was too weak to fight.

I dragged myself through the Christmas holidays in increasingly deep despair, drinking at home and in a neighborhood bar to dull the pain, troubled again by the haunting voices of my mother in my head, voices that I had thought to be stilled forever. The principal at Becahi was well aware of my crisis and tried to help, but at the same time he told me forcefully that I had to "get my act together" before school started in January. I resented what I thought was my principal's insensitivity, at once feeling guilty for my failures and sorry for myself.

Two days before school started at Becahi in January of 1969, I got arrested in Allentown for driving drunk, tossed into the drunk tank for the night so I could drive home sober the next morning. I was suspended from my job at Becahi for one semester and admonished to complete an Alcoholics Anonymous program successfully if I planned to return to Becahi in the fall. I was insulted by the implication that I was an alcoholic, upset that no one seemed to understand that I was drinking excessively only because I was grieving at my abandonment. I swore to myself that I would never take another drink, but I didn't go to AA, and I didn't go back to Becahi. Instead, I resolved to go back to Arizona, determined to exorcise my demons. The carefully constructed edifice of my life was collapsing all about me, and I knew that before I could rebuild, I would have to unearth the foundations of the old life.

CHAPTER 7

Killing

A Greyhound bus had carried me from Arizona to Pennsylvania when I enrolled at Lehigh in 1960, transporting me from one world to another, from a childhood world of fear and doubt to an adult world of promise and optimism. I never imagined that the day would come when I felt compelled to reverse that journey, going backward in space and time, going backward in my state of mind as well.

Once I resolved to return to Arizona, I knew that I could not lose control of my decision by becoming encapsulated in a bus. I knew that I had to drive Lani's MG to Tucson.

Our automobile insurance paid for damage to the other guy, so the Cadillac received a new front grille and minor bodywork. But I could not afford the estimate to repair the extensive damage to the left side of the MG. I paid the

Coyote Speaks

man at the neighborhood gas station to pry the left front fender from its crumpled interference with the tire and then align the wheels, leaving a car in good mechanical condition but with a permanently jammed front door, a window down, and a convertible top locked forever in its mangled storage compartment. I realized that I could jump into the driver's seat over the door with ease, and that was good enough. The car had been paid for by Lani's father, but it was purchased by Lani and registered in her married name, Lani Coyote, so I thought I could probably pass a routine vehicle check, assuming that her father would consider the car totally wrecked and not report it as stolen.

I left Bethlehem in late January of 1969, immediately soaked to the skin by a driving, icy rain; nonetheless feeling liberated in that damaged red roadster with its open top and crushed left door; feeling excited about my decision to retrace my steps, first to Tucson and then to Ajo; and feeling brave about my decision to find and face my childhood demons.

I was not so brave, nor so foolish, as to drive very far south from Bethlehem, fearing that some backwoods cop on one of America's southern roads would stop a brown-skinned man in a damaged red roadster just because he looked out of place. Instead I drove west, traversing

Chapter 7: Killing

Pennsylvania to enter Ohio, moving on to Indiana and Illinois before I began to turn south into Missouri and then Oklahoma, where Indian faces began to appear and my sense of vulnerability faded. I had felt fully justified in taking Lani's car, but I was not ready to face charges as a car thief.

I had been driving very hard for long hours, stopping briefly at rest stops or byways for a nap and then pressing on. But just west of Oklahoma City I stopped in a cheap motel for a good night's sleep. I had no plan when I left Bethlehem and I needed to think with a clear head.

I placed a call to Mama K and announced without explanation that I was coming to Tucson in a few days. Coach and Mama K had not heard from me since my wedding, which I had announced in a long letter filled with self-congratulations on my master's degree, my job, and my marriage. Mama K asked no questions, however, and assured me that a bed would be waiting for me above the garage and she would bake an apple pie in my honor. I did not yet know when I would continue on to Ajo or what I would do there, but I knew I would be welcome in Tucson. I had never known a better home than the Karangetti house and I had never known a better mother than Mama K.

Coyote Speaks

The balance of the trip, through Oklahoma, the Texas Panhandle, New Mexico, and into Arizona, was much more relaxing and actually enjoyable, after days of running scared. I knew I was an Indian among Indians in that part of America, so I could pause to take note of the differences among Native American tribes and observe their varying roles in the surrounding communities. My experience with Indian people was limited to the tribes in Southern Arizona, principally the Tohono O'odham and the Yaqui. Their contrast with tribes as far east as Oklahoma was stark, and even within Arizona I found new perspectives from such different tribes as the Hopi, the Navajo, and the Apache. I was proud to be an Indian, a Native American, but despite my academic explorations at Lehigh, I was naive to the complexities of contemporary Native American cultures, having been immersed in non-Indian environments since the age of five. I vowed that someday I would learn more about my people, but first I had to take care of my own business. That would begin in Tucson.

I arrived in Tucson late in the day, finding both Coach and Mama K at home and glad to see me. We had been apart for more than eight years, so there was much to say that night as we talked and laughed into the early morning

Chapter 7: Killing

hours, but much went unsaid as well. Both Coach and Mama K were perceptive and compassionate people who knew that I would need time to get comfortable before I could talk about the reason I was in Tucson. Before pressing me with questions, they shared their own good news.

Thoroughly Americanized by this time, Kenali Karangetti was "Ken" to most of his American friends, although he was still Dr. Karangetti abroad, where he had earned an international reputation for effective recruiting of runners in Africa and beyond. Coach K had deflected several head coaching job inquiries over the years, accepting elevation at Arizona to associate head coach with top responsibility for the cross country team, recognizing that relocation would compromise his wife's professional career. Only recently he had been promised the job of head coach for track and cross country at the newly established Pima College (later known as Pima Community College), so their patience had been rewarded, with Coach K becoming a head coach without Mama K giving up her high position at Kino Hospital. As a black man with a Hispanic wife, Kenali knew that they both had overcome serious obstacles in achieving their professional aspirations, and his pride was obvious in the telling. When they married in 1946 it would have been illegal in Arizona for either of

Coyote Speaks

them to marry a white person, and their marriage to each other was a violation of social norms in white, black, and Hispanic communities. Despite these external pressures, they made a commitment to each other and made it work far better than most conventional marriages.

Kenali and Teresa felt no less satisfaction as parents. Their son Dominic, always a source of deep pride in the Karangetti family, was about to graduate from the University of Arizona and enter its College of Law. Daughter Kira was now eighteen, following her mother into nursing at her alma mater. While I had a lot to say to Coach K and Mama K, they also bubbled over with news of their own family and the athletes who formed for them an extended family. I was pleased to be counted among the members of that extended family and proud to share with them the goals that I had accomplished in their name.

I was more exhausted, both physically and emotionally, than I had realized, and hungrier, too. Mama K's apple pie served to ease all of those appetites, not just those of my empty belly. I slept most of my first full day in Tucson, awakening to eat and chat a bit, and then to bed again. Mama K didn't rush me; she waited until I was ready to talk.

Chapter 7: Killing

After my second dinner with Coach and Mama K, having declined the glass of wine I would normally have accepted from my hosts, I began by explaining my abstinence. I told my story backward, beginning with the DUI that triggered my decision to drive west, explaining the funk that led to drunk driving by talking about Lani's accident, backing up to confess all my problems with Lani since our marriage. It's not a pretty story, and I felt somehow both guilty and naively foolish in telling it, but with some difficulty I got it all out. As Coach and Mama K quietly absorbed my story, I felt the shame melting away. I was finally ready to talk about my future.

When I asked Coach and Mama K what they knew about the little boy who came to their door more than twelve years earlier, they exchanged knowing glances, seeking consensus before opening up to me. They had decided years ago not to share all they knew about my family background until I was ready for some disturbing information, but clearly this was the time. It seems that Mama K had done some research before accepting into her home the fifteen-year-old boy her husband had taken under his coach's wing at the age of six. They had checked the archives of the *Ajo Copper News* and the back files of the

131

Coyote Speaks

Pima County child welfare agency before taking a chance as my new foster parents, replacing the Durkins.

When Jake and Molly Durkin caught me stealing eggs at their ranch, apparently they called the child welfare agency, where they had longstanding relationships as foster parents, and learned about the fiery car crash that had killed a transient family two days earlier and probably left me unaccountably as the sole survivor. My face was rather badly burned on the left side, and my hair and left sleeve were singed by fire, presumably the fire from that burning car. My origin was no longer a mystery, but my identity was still not at all clear. Apparently I told the Durkins that my name was Joey with no last name given, so they put me on the agency rolls as Joey Kit Coyote. The good people at the child welfare agency arranged for the Durkins to receive and hold for their new foster child a few artifacts surviving the fire, but no papers that would establish my family name. Presumably Jake Durkin still had these items in his possession, things that rightly belonged to me.

Now I knew why I had to return to Ajo. I needed to confront Jake Durkin and reclaim the artifacts of the fire, hoping somehow to piece together the puzzle parts that would define my identity. I had to know where I came from. I had to know my name.

Chapter 7: Killing

The journey by car from Tucson to Ajo is not very long, a couple of hours at most, passing through the Tohono O'odham Reservation to Highway 85 before heading north a dozen more miles to Ajo. It's not long by car, but I drove this route very slowly one late afternoon, trying vainly to remember how I felt when I was running the other way on foot, running from the Durkin chicken ranch into the arms of Mama K.

I could not dredge up specific memories of that long-ago run, but I had no difficulty rekindling the fires that drove me to face such pain. I remembered running with Solo's ghost, remembered digging Solo's grave, remembered Timmy's white face in that bloody bathtub and the look on Aunt Molly's tortured countenance, almost equally pale. I remembered how impotent I felt when The Old Man's shovel knocked me to the ground, how ashamed I was that I shed tears when I really wanted to shed blood.

I wondered how I would feel when I confronted The Old Man at the end of my journey to Ajo. I then knew that Jake Durkin owed me some precious items from the fire's ashes, and I knew that I would get them at any cost.

On the outskirts of Ajo, well after dark, I pulled into a rundown old motel remembered from my years running past it on my way to school. The neon sign said "REST,"

133

Coyote Speaks

with only four letters illuminated, but I remembered the full sign in the daylight reading "EVEREST MOTEL." If this was a poor play on words it was the only evidence of creativity in the proprietress, a hard, pinch-faced white woman known only as Mrs. Hawkins. I sat for a moment or two in my open car, hesitating to enter the mean space Mrs. Hawkins called a lobby. A fine-looking black Chrysler sedan pulled into the parking space next to mine, and the passenger exited on my side, a young woman with full breasts bursting from her low-cut dress and a short skirt that parted to reveal her red panties as she turned in her seat to leave the car, nodding and smiling long lashes at my damaged red roadster, then widening her eyes with a look of recognition.

"Kit!" she cried. "Kit Coyote! What brings you back to Ajo?"

It was Catty, transformed beyond my recognition by the demands of her profession, escorting her john to Cabin #6, the last cabin in the row leading back from the highway. She had a key, and the respectable looking gentleman she led by the arm had no need to register.

"Ask for Cabin #5," she said to me quietly. "The judge has to be home by midnight, so I'll come to Cabin #5 about that time. We've got a lot to talk about."

Chapter 7: Killing

I lay wide-eyed on my too-soft bed in Cabin #5, waiting for Catty's knock on the door, hoping that she would not misconstrue my eagerness to see her. I needed to know what happened on the chicken ranch after I ran away and what would await me if I paid The Old Man a visit the following day.

Catty had looked animated when she guided the judge to their rendezvous in Cabin #6, but when she knocked on my door in Cabin #5 she looked tired and older than the twenty-nine years she claimed. She collapsed on my bed as soon as she entered the room, so I shifted to the adjoining chair, the only chair in the cabin. She closed her eyes "for just a minute," and didn't move for a half-hour as I waited impatiently. When her eyes opened, she winked at me and sat up in the bed, ready to talk.

"I'm 'Cat' now," she purred, "not little Catty anymore. I left the ranch when The Old Man wanted me just for himself, but Pastor Bob wanted me, too. I made my choice and moved out, taking a cabin here at the Everest Motel until Pastor Bob could set me up right.

"His wife got wind o' me and laid him out. Rather than face disgrace with his parishioners, he left me hangin' there. Mrs. Hawkins took me in for a while before she offered me a business proposition: We split my take equally for

135

any john she sets up for me, with a smaller cut for her when I bring in a john of my own, like the judge here, a regular. I've been living here for eight years and will stay until I score big with the right guy."

"What about the others," I said, "about Snow, Mary, and Diego, about Jake and Molly Durkin?"

"Aunt Molly died soon after your run," she said quietly, "and Diego moved out after high school, where he was elected Homecoming King in his senior year and graduated proudly."

She frowned when I pressed her about Snow.

"Little Snow was mad at you when you run away. She said you promised to be her protector and then left her at the mercy of The Old Man, who showed her no mercy at all after Aunt Molly died and I left him for Pastor Bob. Poor, dumb Mary... Jake must have thought she wasn't worth fuckin' and he went right after little Snow."

"So what happened?" I asked Catty. "Where is she now? Can I see her?"

"Snow's dead," she murmured, "Snow's dead."

In her own way, Catty told me about Snow. As I understood Catty, Snow had found her way to the darkest corners of her small community, discovering drugs that would ease her pain, finding other men who wanted

Chapter 7: Killing

what Jake wanted but didn't smell as bad. Catty spoke of men who got a special thrill from Snow's exotic look and childlike vulnerability, the kind of thrill that comes with rape, even when she took their money.

"Snow was a valuable piece of property and men fought to own her. Mrs. Hawkins is my business partner; don't nobody own The Cat."

Catty told me that Snow had died a year ago in a back alley, her frail body broken by an overdose of the drugs that long ago broke her spirit. In Catty's words, "Nobody owns Snow now 'cept maybe God."

Catty assured me that Jake and Mary were still at the ranch, but after learning about Snow my heart was too heavy that night to ask for details about Mary or Jake himself. I fell on the bed close to Catty, and we cried together over old and painful memories until exhaustion overcame us and brought troubled sleep.

I awakened very early the next morning knowing that I would see Jake Durkin just as soon as I could drive the mile or so back south to the ranch. I didn't pause to say farewell to the sleeping Catty, I hurried to my car and raced to the ranch with vengeance in my heart, Snow added to Solo and Timmy as the flash points of my anger, but in truth carrying a deeper resentment at my own exploitation

137

Coyote Speaks

and abuse. When I knocked on the ranch house door that early morning my pulse was pounding, and I had no plan beyond confrontation.

Mary came quickly to the door, her forefinger pressed to her lips in a characteristic gesture. "Shush up," she said, "The Old Man is still sleepin'. Come into the kitchen, Kit. I've been waitin' for you to show up."

Following Mary into that familiar house, sitting at the scarred old wooden table in the kitchen with a mug of coffee and a plate of cornbread soon before me, I marveled at how easily I fell back into a family routine with Mary. She was older, of course, probably thirty, and somewhat thicker in the middle, but she still moved in a sure-footed way, strong and steady, seeming to be a survivor in her role as The Old Man's entire support system.

Seated at the table I could see the kitchen door that led across the living room to The Old Man's bedroom, so I was alert to the possibility that Jake could interrupt us at any moment, but I wanted Mary to myself for a bit longer. I wanted to confront the man she was living with, but first I needed to better understand their relationship.

Obviously the chicken ranch was not the functioning operation that I remembered, with Molly and the seven

Chapter 7: Killing

foster children reduced now to just Mary, but that seemed to be of no concern.

"Jake is cutting back his chicken population, selling more to local restaurants and markets and delivering eggs to fewer customers, boasting that he has more money put aside than he would ever need."

"Put away where?" I wondered aloud.

"That old red trunk with the brass padlock is Jake's only bank," she said, "and lately he's been taking more out than he is putting in.

"Jake spends hours alone in the garage, probably savoring his riches in that trunk, which obviously includes his stash of whiskey as well, judging by the smell of the man when he comes back into the house." Mary was describing Jake's behavior almost clinically, with neither affection nor contempt.

When I asked how she was doing personally, she responded initially with similar passivity, talking quietly but at some length about her friends and family on the reservation and her life on the ranch after all the other foster children had moved on. The only emotion Mary displayed was in response to my question about children. She shakily acknowledged one pregnancy that resulted in

Coyote Speaks

a stillborn delivery at home, saying that she now always carries a knife and had to use it one night to fend off his drunken assault.

"I cut his hand deep that night, and he never come after me again. He knew me then as a light sleeper with a sharp knife."

Mary didn't quite say that Jake was responsible for her pregnancy, but it seemed to me to be clear that there was no other man in her life. What was not so clear was why she stayed on the ranch, or what other options she had in life. She was talking to me openly about Jake's personal life, but still her apprehensive glances at the door as she paced the floor told me that she was taking a risk in talking to me. She said that after her baby died and she denied Jake her bed he had in his jealousy sworn to shoot any other man who visited her in his house, and she knew that we would both be in danger if he saw my car parked outside.

Jake's roar and his pounding boots on the wooden floor announced his presence even before he kicked open the kitchen door, giving me the full second I needed to escape the blast of The Old Man's shotgun by knocking over the kitchen table and falling to my belly behind it. Mary watched, her mouth agape, as Jake came around the table, the forefinger of his right hand on the second trigger

Chapter 7: Killing

of that old double-barreled shotgun. But every cultivated instinct I had developed as a wrestler told me to charge the gun, not to try to hide from it again. I grabbed the barrel with my right hand, pulling it toward me and pushing it up as the gun discharged into the ceiling, and with my left hand I pushed up Jake's right elbow, ducking under that arm and spinning around to his back. (Wrestlers call this move the "duck under," not my best move on the mat, but good enough for Jake.)

The Old Man still stood above me a good four inches taller, and he was probably sixty pounds heavier. From behind, I had to jump onto Jake's back, my knees pressed against his ample midriff, so I could encircle his neck with my left arm, the hard bone of my forearm pressed against his throat, simultaneously throwing my right arm over Jake's right shoulder so I could grip my inner right elbow with my left hand and with my right hand apply great pressure to the back of The Old Man's head, which he turned slightly to his left, trying to escape my grip. I heard my wrestling coach hollering at me for using the illegal "hangman's grip," but the coach was calling from a different world.

My actions were purely reflexive, muscle memory executed rapidly while Jake was thrashing about, trying

Coyote Speaks

to fight me off with the butt of his empty gun; banging my head and body against the wall and then falling on his back with me still clinging there; hammered to the floor by Jake's great weight, gasping for air but at the same time extending my long legs to wrap tightly around Jake's ribs, above the great expanse of his belly, crossing my ankles to lock the hold. I took a deep breath and then flexed every muscle, squeezing my legs to stretch out his body, tightening my left arm at Jake's throat and, most critically, forcing the back of Jake's head toward his chest until I heard the loud crack that told me I had broken The Old Man's neck. Jake Durkin was dead in the arms of Kit Coyote.

As I looked up from under Jake's lifeless body I saw Mary coming at me with a knife, drawn from some hidden place on her person, and I thought from her tight frown that I was in trouble. She quickly and adroitly severed the leather thong around Jake's neck, however, took possession of the little brass key The Old Man always carried, and whispered in my ear, "He needed killin'. I'm glad it was you, my little Kit. I'm glad it was you who finally got to take him down."

The hour that followed was even then blurry in my mind, my head bruised from hitting the wall and my

Chapter 7: Killing

brain numb from the realization of my violence, which was entirely foreign to my sense of myself. I had killed a man with the conditioned reflex of a seasoned wrestler, ferociously and with adrenaline flowing, but without fear or anger, indeed without any emotion at all. Only in the wake of the killing could I smell the stench of The Old Man as his bowels greeted his death. Only then could I hear the sickening crack of Jake's spine as his scrawny neck gave way to my leveraged force. Only then did I want to cry in my weakness, as I did many years ago when Jake's shovel knocked me to the ground. At least this time I stood up to The Old Man.

Mary was thinking clearly, however, and she led me to the garage, unlocked the red trunk, and began sorting out its contents on the concrete floor. The old trunk was more than a foot deep with a floor maybe two feet by three feet, a large enough volume to store all kinds of stuff valued by The Old Man. Mary's first items from the trunk were liquor bottles, all Jack Daniel's Tennessee Sour Mash Whiskey, four full and one half-empty. She removed a small flour sack tied securely at the top, setting it aside while she removed four shoe boxes, each tied with a shoe lace of a different color: red, white, blue and gold. At the bottom of the trunk was a formal black suit in a plastic

143

Coyote Speaks

bag and what appeared to be a wedding gown in another. Finally, there were two slender photo albums, each filled with faded Kodak prints in black and white. Mary and I realized that we might as well be looking at the ashes of Jake and Molly Durkin.

Mary opened the shoe boxes, untying shoe laces that had clearly been loosely tied and untied many times before, boxes containing paper money, bills of different denominations in each: $5, $10, $20, and $50 bills. In each box the bills were collected in packets encircled by large rubber bands, some brittle with age, maybe a hundred bills in each packet. Quickly riffling through the fifty-dollar box, counting not the individual bills but the packets, she estimated $40,000 in that box alone, assembled in eight packets. We were in possession of Jake's retirement money, but for Mary and me it was blood money. Mary started doling it all out in two piles, clearly signaling one for me and one for herself. She distributed the packets of currency and didn't then take the time to count the money; she produced two green garbage bags and handed one to me.

The other mystery to be solved was the small flour sack, which I hoped might contain the promised artifacts from my family's car fire, things I deserved to have as my own. We were afraid to take the time needed to confirm

Chapter 7: Killing

this expectation, saving my exploration of the contents for a time when we didn't have a dead body in the kitchen.

When Mary and I got back in the house, she yanked the telephone wire from the wall and began explaining to me what we must do with a clarity that suggested the execution of a plan developed over months or years of scheming. She began by insisting that I slap her hard on the mouth, hard enough to draw blood. She laughed at my first attempt and asked for another, harder hit, not satisfied until she could taste the blood that ran down her chin. This was hard for me, harder than breaking Jake's neck; I don't hit women, ever. Mary then sat on a kitchen chair and loosely bound her ankles to the chair's front legs, handing me strips of white cloth she tore from an old kitchen towel, urging me to tie her wrists together securely behind the back of the chair, which I did without yet understanding her intentions.

"Now watch me," she said, "to be sure that I can get my legs free without help."

She began rocking the chair, increasing her effort until the chair toppled over backward, her head hitting the floor with a great thud. Smiling, she kicked the telephone wire loops off the ends of the chair legs and struggled to her feet, extracting her arms from the chair back but not

145

Coyote Speaks

loosening her bonds. She was now free to walk with her hands tied behind her, bloodied and bound as a victim would be. Mary then shocked me with a hard kiss, murmured something about my avenging her lost baby, and told me forcefully to tie a gag around her mouth (but not her nose) and take my new belongings to California in my "funny little car." She supposed that she would take a nap of an hour or two and then begin the long walk to Ajo. She was offering me time to make my escape and at the same time protecting herself from any suspicion of complicity in Jake Durkin's murder.

Clever girl, my Mary… clever girl… not so slow after all. Somehow her tormentor is dead and she goes home with half of his life savings, all free of any risk of punishment. How did she know I was coming?

It was not yet noon when I drove the MG from the yard of the chicken ranch, knowing I would never return. I was exhilarated and at the same time terrified, proud of myself for finally confronting my tormentor and at the same time ashamed of killing a man, fearing that I would eventually be punished for my crime. My mind was in confusion, but there was one thing I did understand: I must run as hard and as fast as I had ever run before.

Chapter 7: Killing

As I raced down the highway I felt again the "out-of-body" sensation that I first experienced in the AAU Cross Country Championships, as though I was looking down on a runner in pain but not feeling the pain myself. I knew that I had killed a man with my bare hands, and I knew that was wrong, but suffering in remorse was confined to the runner and not something I felt at a higher level, where I was plotting my escape and trying to keep the driver from exceeding the speed limit.

As Mary advised me, I ran to California, heading for Los Angeles where an Indian fugitive could hope to hide forever. I didn't stop to count my blood money or to investigate the promises in the flour sack. I drove until I crossed the Colorado River at the California border and only then began to quiet my nerves and look for a place to rest. I stopped in a Holiday Inn on the highway near Indio, on the southern end of the string of desert towns that leads finally to LA.

CHAPTER 8

The Hard Road Home

I carried that green garbage bag full of Jake's money into my room at the Holiday Inn, double-locked the door, closed the blinds, and took a deep breath. This was blood money, stolen from a man whose life, however mean, I had taken from him. It's true that Jake aimed to kill me with that shotgun, just as he had killed Solo more than ten years earlier. It's true that he repeatedly abused Catty, Snow, and Mary as young girls; sending Catty and Snow on the path to prostitution and driving Snow to her death, just as his wife had driven Timmy to suicide even earlier. I escaped the worst abuses suffered by Jake's foster children because I found sponsors at school and then escaped to their care, but I too was exploited and mistreated during the ten years I survived on the chicken ranch. As Mary

Coyote Speaks

said, "He needed killin'," but I wondered, *Was I the one to kill him? And what will happen to me now? Must I hide from the authorities for the rest of my life, changing my good name and relinquishing my hard-earned educational credentials? Can I ever be a teacher again, doing what I love?*

No matter how much money I might find in that garbage bag, I knew that it couldn't be enough to pay for the sacrifice of the good life I once enjoyed in Pennsylvania. If killing Jake was worthwhile, it must be for the satisfaction of revenge, not for the financial reward.

Still, I knew I had to count the money and decide what to do with it. As I touched the money I saw the hands of the man I had killed, knowing that this was his money, not mine. I knew that Jake had salted this money away in his red chest week by week for thirty years, savoring the day when he could rest easy with the riches of a lifetime. Yet now it was mine, and I had to force myself to use it wisely.

I counted the packets first. Assuming each packet held one hundred bills, they totaled $32,000. When finally I actually counted the individual bills, noting that some packets were short of 100, I had a total of $30,255.

So what should I do with this money? Twenty-seven years old at the time, I had to find a way to use the money

Chapter 8: The Hard Road Home

to prepare myself to make a living and not allow it to slip away while I remained in hiding.

But I had to wonder, "Who am I?" Joey Kit Coyote had a master's degree and Pennsylvania credentials as a high school teacher, but Kit Coyote was wanted for murder. *Do I have to start over again with a different name? How can I do that?*

I dared to believe that I would find some answers in the flour sack. I found myself hoping against all odds that the mystery of my original identity would somehow reveal itself in the contents of that benign-looking sack, labeled for flour.

The top of the sack was tied so tightly I could not get it open with just my fingers, finally reverting to my teeth to loosen the knot. Jake had apparently not given any recent attention to its contents. Probably he had briefly checked the sack when it was given to him by the county and found nothing of interest to him, tying it back tight in the honest expectation that he would give it to me when I "graduated" from the ranch. When I ran away at fifteen, Jake probably took no further notice of the flour sack in his chest.

The sack contained five items: A large yellow envelope and four small drawstring bags. The envelope got my attention first.

151

Coyote Speaks

Inside the large envelope were two newspaper clippings from the *Ajo Copper News* and a smaller, semi-transparent envelope containing an eight-inch by five-inch photograph.

The larger of the two clippings was dated August 15, 1946, and headlined "Fiery Crash Kills Family," with a small and blurry photo of the wreck included. The story was brief but painful for me to read: "An aging two-door Ford sedan southbound with California license plates tumbled and rolled repeatedly, bursting into flames on Highway 85. Northbound and southbound vehicle skid marks indicate the involvement also of a northbound vehicle with four tires on the rear axle, presumably a truck, but it did not remain at the scene of the accident. Two adults, a man and a woman clutching a silver cross, were burned beyond recognition, as was a teenage boy in the back seat, which was dislodged as the car tumbled. Fierce flames destroyed all evidence of the identity of the family members, except possibly for four items of jewelry."

I hoped that the "four items of jewelry" would be found in the four drawstring bags, but before checking I read the second clipping, which was dated August 19, 1946, and very short. "Boy survives car fire" was the headline, and the text said simply: "A small child escaped from the car fire that took the lives of a transient family last week,

Chapter 8: The Hard Road Home

unaccountably hiding from authorities until he was found at the Durkin ranch. The boy calls himself 'Joey' but offers no further identification. The Durkin family has agreed to accept him as a foster child."

I found no surprises in the second clipping beyond the affirmation that they did know that my name was Joey, not Kit. I still had the evidence in that belt buckle with "JOEY" printed on the metal belt loop, although I had transferred it to a bigger belt when I outgrew the original. The dirty and singed clothing I was wearing when The Old Man found me disappeared within days, so this old belt buckle was the only thing I had from my life before the chicken ranch. I had treasured it always, but now it had special significance.

Next I took the photo from its envelope, recognizing it as a blown-up and sharper version of the car wreck photo reproduced in the first news clipping. What struck me immediately as I stared at that fire-blackened car lying on its side was the open trunk. I shuddered as memories flooded through my mind, memories that had been suppressed for more than twenty years. I saw myself inside that trunk kicking open the broken trunk lid that had been tied down with cotton rope, smelling fresh air but then turning back to call my brother Jimmy, who had pried

153

Coyote Speaks

open the narrow passage that I had used to get into the trunk from the backseat, a passage too tight for Jimmy.

Jimmy yelled at me in a voice I heard over my mother's screams, a voice I had always remembered from my childhood: "Run, Joey, hide. Go now!"

As I stuck my head back into the narrow space opened by the dislodged back seat to hear Jimmy, the entire car shuddered and the seat shifted to close the passageway, pressing the burning seat cushion painfully against me, searing my face. I pulled back hard, crawled out of the trunk, and ran; not stopping when I heard the car explode behind me; dropping into a roadside ditch when other cars drove by; then running again, running hard, the sounds of my mother's screams reverberating in my brain, my brother's voice telling me to run and hide.

I lay down in that bed in the Indio Holiday Inn, exhausted by reliving that fire, relieved by the lifting of the veil from my memory, satisfied that finally I knew how I got to the chicken ranch all alone. However, I still didn't know my full name.

Would the artifacts of the fire in those four little drawstring bags hold the answer to that final question?

The first bag held a brass belt buckle exactly like mine, except the name on the metal belt loop was "JIMMY." I

Chapter 8: The Hard Road Home

found myself holding a tangible memory of my lost brother, the brother who had saved my life. Memories of Jimmy came flooding back, his smiling eyes and silly grin defining a new image for my brother in my mind, displacing the terror of his voice in that burning car. I then remembered Jimmy as much bigger than I was, trying to teach his little brother how to dribble a soccer ball and ride a bike, bold and self-assured until I saw him kiss a girl under the old mesquite tree behind our house, then suddenly shy and embarrassed (hoping I wouldn't tell anyone). Jimmy was my big brother and the hero of my childhood.

The second bag held a man's copper bracelet, scarred by the fire, but concealed under the soot on the inside were engraved letters, initials not easily interpreted without careful scrubbing, but finally revealing the following: "J.R. Hyde." This was my father's bracelet, and his last name was "Hyde." Somehow this was not a surprise to me; the name "Hyde" had a familiar ring to it. I was very happy to know that I was once Joey Hyde. Wasn't that what my brother called me at the fire? I remembered "Joey, hide!" but now I could hear his words as "Joey Hyde."

Memories of my father that loomed for me were somehow sensory, feeling the exhilaration of being lifted high overhead and at other more quiet times smelling the pipe

Coyote Speaks

tobacco in the ritualistic progression from the fresh scent of his pouch to the newly lit pipe to the slightly acrid smell of the abandoned pipe when the smoking was done. I remembered clearly my father's presence but not his words, which may have been few.

Two drawstring bags remained, and I opened the first of them slowly. What more could I learn?

This third bag held a small, gold wedding band with no inscription, disappointingly barren of any identification.

Only one bag remained, and I struggled with its tight knot, my fingers shaking. When I finally got it open with my teeth, I found within it a silver cross, darkened with age and fire, retrieved, according to the news clipping, from the dead hands of my mother, who was no longer screaming in my ears. Maybe now, I thought, maybe now I can find new memories of my mother to displace the screams that have always filled my head. I allowed my mind to wander into the past, feeling rather than seeing her presence; hearing the songs she sang to her baby in her mother tongue, absorbing the warmth of her voice and her body. I knew then that I could put the screams away in a buried place, hearing instead her quiet songs, her soothing voice whispered in my ears, hearing love rather than fear. I knew then that my wounds could heal.

Chapter 8: The Hard Road Home

Using mild soap in the motel bathroom I scrubbed the silver cross, which was clean on its face and engraved both horizontally and vertically on the back. It read MARIA horizontally and MORONGO vertically, the middle "R" of MARIA shared by the third letter of MORONGO. So her name was Maria, a familiar resonance, but I had no frame of reference for Morongo. Maybe Morongo was her maiden name, so she was once Maria Morongo.

After my discoveries in Indio, I knew my name and enough of my history to remove or at least diminish my fears and anxieties about myself. I was still a fugitive from the law, but I had established a true identity for myself. Now I needed a plan to go forward with a new name but had no credentials on which to build a new life.

I still believed that in the complex and cosmopolitan environment of Los Angeles I could best explore my possibilities. Surely in LA I would be able to buy whatever false credentials I would need to begin a new life as Joey Hyde.

With the motel blinds closed and my body and soul exhausted, I slept late the next morning, surprised that my watch said 10:00 a.m. when I opened my eyes. I quickly ate my free breakfast, paid my bill with cash, and jumped into my little car, heading north on Interstate 10, then a new highway that led directly into Los Angeles.

Coyote Speaks

Less than an hour north of Indio my eye caught an exit sign with a stunning revelation; the sign said "Morongo Indian Reservation." My mother's maiden name was not Maria Morongo: her name was Maria, and Morongo was the name of her tribe.

I had driven past the Morongo exit before my brain processed the implications of the sign, but I left the freeway at the next exit and returned to the reservation by side streets. I found my way to the reservation's main office and, hesitating at the door, drew a deep breath and crossed the threshold.

The harried woman seated at the only desk was trying to quiet a roomful of young people clamoring for her attention, all anxious to get her signature on some kind of form so they could catch the bus waiting outside. The bus driver was periodically honking his horn impatiently. I sat down on a hard chair in the corner and waited for my turn, trying to sort through my thoughts and rehearse my introduction.

When the room cleared I began to see the official at the desk in a new light. She was probably in her fifties, well groomed and finally smiling comfortably as she beckoned me to her desk, apologizing for the chaos, shrugging at the antics of young people.

Chapter 8: The Hard Road Home

I began with the news clippings, then showed her the two brass belt buckles, finally sharing with her the copper bracelet and the silver cross bearing the name Morongo, telling my story with trembling voice. She nodded sympathetically, stopped me before I got beyond the chicken ranch, and picked up her telephone. After a brief conversation beyond my hearing, she pulled a thin folder from the voluminous filing cabinets behind her desk, beckoning me then to collect my stuff and follow her. In no more than a minute we entered the Office of the Tribal Chairman, greeted by an elderly, white-haired gentleman who stood up politely as I entered the room. The three of us spent a full hour together, the chairman confirming not only from tribal records but from his personal memories the presence twenty-odd years ago of the Hyde family: Joseph, Maria, Jimmy, and Joey. He told me, calling me Joey, that my mother had been widowed by the violent death of her first husband, James Jackson, who expired in a trailer fire from which she escaped with her infant son Jimmy; unable to drag from the burning trailer her very large husband, who was too drunk to make it out on his own. She was traumatized by that fire and slow to recover until she met Joseph Hyde, a sober and quiet man who worked hard to care for his

Coyote Speaks

family. In their marriage they created me as their child, sharing my father's name. Jimmy was therefore formally my half-brother, ten years older, but my protector, my champion, and my guide in childhood even more than my father had been. Both of my mother's husbands were born on the Morongo reservation, but she was born as Maria Jasmin Alto to a Yaqui Indian family in northern Mexico. Apparently the Hyde family left the reservation in August of 1946 on a trip to visit my mother's people in Mexico, and they were never heard from again.

The chairman did not question the evidence that I was Joey Hyde and he assured me that they would promptly provide me with a proper ID card and enrollment as a member of the tribe. They even offered to find me temporary lodgings on the reservation for that night at least.

There were tears in my eyes as I received the generous blessings of the tribal chairman, but I didn't break down in heavy sobs until I was alone in my assigned room. Finally, Kit Coyote was at home where he belonged, a man with a proper name and a very large family in this tribal community.

Before I put my past entirely behind me I felt obliged to risk everything in order to say goodbye to Coach and Mama K, who would think me dead if I disappeared

Chapter 8: The Hard Road Home

from their lives without a word. I took the precautions of driving north to the outskirts of Los Angeles and using a pay phone outside of a gas station, but I did place a phone call to their house soon after I had found my childhood home with the Morongos.

I had carefully rehearsed my opening words for Coach and Mama K, so I mumbled incoherently when Kira answered the phone. I finally said "Yes" when she asked if I wanted to speak with her mother. She asked my name and reacted excitedly to my response: "Oh, she's been worried about you."

I told Mama K that I had to disappear because I broke Jake Durkin's neck when Jake came at me with his shotgun, the same weapon he had used to kill Solo. I didn't tell her about the blood money, which caused me greater shame than the killing. I brushed aside her insistence that self-defense is not murder, her attempt to persuade me to go to the authorities with my explanations. I knew that the courts would not look favorably on my presence in the house of a man I had reasons to hate, not to mention my complicity in stealing his money. I quieted her objections, thanked her sincerely for all that she and her husband had done for me, assured her that I was safe and happy in my new home, and said goodbye. Then, for the

161

Coyote Speaks

first time, I said "I love you." I hung up the phone, tears welling in my eyes.

The path ahead of me was crystal clear after I discovered my heritage and settled in to my new identity: I needed to enter school under the name Joseph C. Hyde, earn again the necessary credentials, and try again to become a teacher. That was the work I loved, and I was still young enough to start over again and recapture this opportunity. I had done it all before when I had many distractions. I was sure that I could do it again and do it faster and better.

I completed sixty units in twelve months at Riverside Community College, earning some credits simply by examination, enrolling then as an English major at the University of California, Riverside. Two years later I had my bachelor's degree and the credits required for a California secondary teaching credential, obtained soon thereafter.

The money I once uncomfortably characterized as "blood money" was the key to my ability to become a full-time student for three years, so I no longer harbored any regrets about that money. In fact, I no longer harbored any regrets about my life. Memories of my mother became focused on the soothing sounds of her singing voice and her silver cross, which had provided the clue to my Morongo

Chapter 8: The Hard Road Home

heritage. No longer did I hear her screams. I was ready to earn my credentials again, find a teaching job and rebuild my life, breathing freely for the first time in memory.

For three years I lived with the knowledge that the only thing connecting me to my felonious past was Lani's MG, the damaged red roadster that had carried me faithfully from Pennsylvania to California via Tucson and Ajo. The car was registered in the name Lani Coyote, the last name of a fugitive from the law but not my own name, so I didn't own it, couldn't sell it and couldn't even reregister the car when its registration expired.

However, I needed a car and I couldn't buy another without dangerously depleting Jake's blood money, which had to last until I had credentials in my new name to teach. Besides all that, I really loved that little red car, as small and as damaged as her driver and very much my own.

As I was repeating my studies for the teaching credential I was quite conscious of the red flag that I was waving before every police officer just by driving by, an Indian in a damaged red roadster that wouldn't pass the standard "show me your registration" test.

These fears, like so many others in my life, were groundless. When after about four years I could afford to buy another car with cash, I removed Lani's registration

Coyote Speaks

and drove her car late at night to the closed gate of a junk dealer in a rural area, left the keys in the car, and said my sad farewells with a kiss on her hood.

My parting with the red roadster was a final goodbye to my past identity, warranting a celebration of some kind. My brief struggle with alcohol was almost five years behind me, associated in my mind with grief and not with celebration. I walked past a roadside bar as I hiked home from the resting place of my red roadster, impulsively dropping into the darkness of that cool bar for a quick nip of celebratory vodka. I enjoyed a tall Vodka Collins, savoring every drop and chewing on my lime, wondering if I should top it off with one shot of straight vodka. One drink then seemed hardly sufficient for the occasion, and two led to three. It was closing time when the proprietor shoved me out the door, sending me stumbling into the early morning darkness.

I crawled under a bush by the side of the road and collapsed both physically and mentally, awakening to sunshine and the happy voices of school children walking by, their laughter suddenly stilled when they saw me, their voices dropping to whispers. I caught the words "another drunken Indian… passed out on the road," words that hurt me more than the hangover, words that filled my

Chapter 8: The Hard Road Home

heart with revulsion and shame. I hated myself not only for my weakness but also for being seen by children in such disgusting condition when I wanted above all else to set standards for them to emulate. I accepted for the first time that anguished morning that I am an alcoholic and will be an alcoholic for my lifetime.

When I opened my eyes to the need for help I found meetings of Alcoholics Anonymous readily available and welcoming of one more fellow who was willing to accept reality, back away from the scary edge of the precipice, and deal with a serious illness constructively. I went through the AA process and learned a great deal about myself, establishing a foundation has that kept me clean and sober for all my years. I still drop into AA meetings occasionally, just to renew my commitments and encourage others to believe in their own capacity for recovery (but not cure).

I was honored to be engaged as a high school English teacher under the name Joseph C. Hyde in the town of Banning, just north of the Morongo Reservation, and devoted myself to this responsibility for a full career, also

Coyote Speaks

volunteering in the early years as an assistant coach for both track and wrestling. I simply loved being a teacher.

I made the mistake of telling the head track coach that as a young runner I bore the nickname "Coyote," which the coach insisted on using publicly thereafter, with the nickname soon adopted by the entire athletic department and then spreading to the faculty (and to the students beyond my presence).

Many of my friends and associates began to believe that out of my Indian heritage my middle initial "C" stood for "Coyote," not Charles, and they began to call me by what they regarded as my middle name. I became again Coyote, just as I was in my former life, just as I was as a boy. I came to like the name, which I now carry proudly.

I was in my midthirties when my friendship with Anna Czova, the Banning High School librarian, matured into a love different from and deeper than the infatuation that drew me as a very young man to the beautiful Lani Beckman.

Although Anna was thirty when we married, having accepted her role as a spinster librarian, she seemed to me to embody all the compellingly attractive human qualities that I remembered so dearly in Miss Hunkin, the Sunnyside High School librarian of my youth, and the

Chapter 8: The Hard Road Home

trim figure that she inherited from her Chinese-American mother added to her appeal.

Anna told me that her father, Zdenic Czova, was a Czech refugee at the outset of World War II, a professor of medieval history at Charles University in Prague when Hitler's panzers invaded Czechoslovakia; fortunately at a time when Professor Czova was attending an international conference at the University of California in Berkeley. Both his mother and his wife back in Prague were ethnically Jewish, although not practicing the faith, and Zdenic knew immediately that neither they nor he would be safe from the Nazi purges that were then widely reported. Zdenic made the practical decision to cancel his flight home, saving himself by successfully seeking refugee status and eventually becoming a US citizen. His efforts to contact his family in Prague after the war were predictably fruitless.

A temporary academic appointment at Cal Berkeley led to a job at the campus bookstore and finally to a small bookstore of his own near Chinatown in San Francisco, a place he called Global Books.

Anna seemed to want to share with me the details of her father's story, although the linkage to her mother was in some ways a sad affair.

Coyote Speaks

Anna's mother was a third-generation Chinese-American named Emily Chu, educated at Cal Berkeley and UC San Francisco medical school; a physician whose clientele were primarily but not exclusively residents of San Francisco's Chinatown. She loved to prowl through bookstores in the bay area, and she discovered not only Global Books but an exciting Czech émigré named Zdenic Czova, who shared her love of international literature as well as her taste for radical politics. In his youth Zdenic was not quite a Communist, and the occupation of his Czech homeland by the Soviets moved him irrevocably from that ideology. But he remained spiritually committed to an ideal vision of human destiny that Emily shared. She also shared his bed, and her pregnancy with Anna led to a marriage that was vigorously opposed by her traditional Chinese parents. Their marriage lasted only two years, and Anna was raised by her mother in a social environment that left the child isolated and insecure.

Anna's refuge was in her love of books, a passion she shared with both of her separated parents. Her mother's medical practice supported Anna through nine years at Cal Berkeley, culminating in a PhD in American Literature and no job. Determined to end her dependence on her mother, she moved to Los Angeles and enrolled at UCLA

168

Chapter 8: The Hard Road Home

for a master's degree in library science. She accepted the high school librarian's job in Banning as a way station to greater things; but for the first time in her life she felt valued by the students whose lives she could influence for the good.

Anna was settled in her job and reasonably content with the compromises in her life until I joined her on the Banning High School faculty. We discovered each other as two lost souls, coming together first intellectually, then emotionally, and finally in unfamiliar intimacy. Even then Anna allowed me to shield her from the darkest secrets of my past.

Our marriage was a blessing for both of us, even without children, and we lived together in the Banning area for more than thirty years. Sadly, ovarian cancer took her from me too soon, but we celebrated life together until the very end.

My own time on this earth is coming to an end as pancreatic cancer takes its toll, but I feel truly content. I found a second life as a member of the Morongo community, so I will die where I was born. I do regret that the wall created by the status of Kit Coyote as a fugitive has kept me from reaching across this barrier to thank those good people who helped me as Kit Coyote survive and then succeed.

169

Coyote Speaks

But I knew I could not do more myself than I accomplished with that one phone call to Mama K. Life is never simple and it's not always fair; neat solutions cannot always be found for human problems. I always tried hard to accept life as I found it, grateful for its blessings and resilient in response to its adversities.

BOOK II

Another Perspective

CHAPTER 9

The Witness

She noticed the Indian kid from Arizona even before the race began. He stood awkwardly at the starting line on a cross-country course at Lehigh University in Bethlehem, Pennsylvania, a race that would determine the AAU national champion for boys under nineteen. Having lost his breakfast on the field just before the race, he was still feeling light-headed and a bit dizzy as he glanced nervously at his fellow runners, waiting for the starter's gun. She imagined that he would look pale if not for the rich brown skin that concealed his fear, brown except for a white patch on his left cheek that might have been a burn scar. His long arms and legs seemed loosely connected to a thick torso with a deep chest, all contributing to an impression of ungainliness, like a young colt, not yet strong enough

Coyote Speaks

for a long race. The boy was smaller than most of the runners in that field; he went by the name Kit Coyote.

Although he got off to a rough start, jostled by the runners at his side, in less than a minute it became clear to her that this kid was settling into a stride that would take him to a gold ring if he could sustain it. As a seasoned reporter for *RUNNERS Journal* Andrea Parker had witnessed cross country competition at all levels, analyzing the world's best distance runners, and she felt sure she could identify a winning stride. Most runners bounced up and down as they ran, but Kit's head and shoulders rose and fell only as the terrain demanded. When his speed increased his arms and legs moved faster, but his head and torso were unchanged, his breathing steady and strong, his expression at ease once the race began. Although his speed changed with the terrain, every stride seemed equally easy.

Andrea was a Texas girl, and she had seen coyote running wild with a natural gait that could cover any distance with no apparent effort. Kit Coyote brought that image to her mind. Was this his real name?

Whatever his true name, she knew he would win this race even as he fought for running room in the middle of the pack.

Chapter 9: The Witness

Although Andrea anticipated the outcome of the cross country race, she was shocked after the race to hear talk of the fate of the winner as a victim of a devastating, fiery collision of his bus with a large truck on Highway 22. Rumors were flying and all passengers were initially reported dead, but as she reached the scene of the accident she found a few survivors, including the Indian boy she had found so interesting. Andrea followed the ambulance carrying Kit Coyote to the hospital, hoping to verify the street talk of his heroism. Her casual interest in this young man was becoming a serious fascination, and she was determined to learn more.

Kit was released from the hospital with minor bruises and burns on his hands and face; released to join the crowd of runners, coaches and families gathered in the hospital lobby, anxious people not yet ready to return to their empty hotel rooms. The President of Lehigh University was there, among those shaking Kit's hand and calling him a hero. But he was grateful when a friendly woman with an air of authority took his arm, acknowledging his exhaustion and offering to drive him to his hotel for some much needed rest. Kit didn't question her motives and didn't discover that Andrea was a reporter until they were in her car.

Coyote Speaks

She was in Bethlehem to cover the AAU cross country meet, she told Kit, and that would be routinely reported in the next edition of *RUNNERS Journal*. But she also had another assignment from her editor, who was cowriting a book with her about young runners and their motivations, including lengthy character sketches about runners with unusual personal histories. Andrea told Kit she wanted to hear his story.

"You are different, Kit, in so many ways. You have a God-given talent as a runner, but that's not enough to take you to this level as a competitor. When did you become a runner, and why? What's the secret of your success?"

"Coach K."

"Okay, so Coach K has helped you to develop your talents, but no coach can teach you to run as you do."

"Coach K saved my life."

Now Andrea's curiosity was engaged. "How did he save your life?"

Kit paused, not sure he wanted to go further. Finally he said, "Coach and Mama K rescued me from the chicken ranch."

As an experienced reporter, Andrea was never at a loss for the next question, but she realized that she was in sensitive territory, so she said nothing as they entered

Chapter 9: The Witness

the hotel parking lot and walked together into the lobby. As Kit turned to thank her for the ride, she surrendered to her impulses.

"I need to know more about you, Kit. How can I do that? May I go with you to your room and talk about the chicken ranch?"

Kit didn't know what to say or do. He was grateful to Andrea for her kindness and touched by her interest in his personal story; he didn't want to be rude or appear arrogant. But Kit never talked about the chicken ranch with anyone, and Andrea was a total stranger. She had a very appealing way about her, though, chatting during their twenty-minute drive together about her own experience as first a distance runner at the University of Texas, then an assistant coach, and finally a sports reporter. She told him that most distance runners hit their peaks in their late twenties or early thirties, so he should look forward to continuous improvement for many years if he stayed healthy and worked hard under the right coaches. She made him feel good about himself and Kit believed that he could trust her to hear his story with understanding and compassion. Anyway, he was too tired to resist her eager insistence and too wired to go to his room just to sleep.

177

Coyote Speaks

So Kit sat down in his hotel room and talked to Andrea and her tape recorder. He was initially hesitant, as he stumbled over such unexpected questions as "Why do you run?" but once he got started his words came in a torrent, words that had been bottled up for many years, words that freed him from suppressed memories, speaking for hours.

Andrea had no way of knowing that in writing Kit's story she would someday provide a link between Coyote as an old man and a University of Arizona grad student named Sarah Whitewater, a young woman who would one day lift a great burden from the shoulders of Coyote Viejo with the best news he could imagine.

CHAPTER 10

Sarah Whitewater

Her father told her she would be in over her head as an affirmative action freshman at Stanford, admitted only because of her Cherokee heritage as an Oklahoma girl from Stillwater who qualified for the Stanford track team. Sarah was anxious to prove him wrong, to prove that she was smart enough and strong enough to survive anywhere. But she was scared.

Sarah knew that her father resented her decision to leave home when she had a perfectly fine university right in her own backyard; a university that was good enough for her brother Jack and both of her parents, a university where her father taught petroleum engineering, so her tuition would be waived. But with Jack's encouragement

Coyote Speaks

she had decided to break out on her own and show her parents that she deserved their respect.

When she accepted her admission to Stanford as a liberal arts student with a partial scholarship in the fall of 2003 she was determined to define her own standards of achievement and march to her own drummer; immersing herself in an intellectual and personal adventure that left her technically oriented and technically educated parents and brother behind; forging her own discipline through cross country running and a very demanding academic curriculum in a highly competitive learning environment. Stanford is a great university for science and engineering, her father acknowledged, but Sarah believed it was also a place where the arts and humanities could flourish.

Actually Stanford was exactly the right place for Sarah, but her parents thought the jump from Stillwater, Oklahoma, would be too much for her, and at first she feared that they might be right.

As a freshman Sarah enrolled in a World Civilizations class that offered her a wholly new perspective on humanity. Stanford's academic calendar has four quarters, including summer, and for the fall quarter her World Civ class met in a section of thirty students three times a week with young Professor Karinski, who covered another section as

Chapter 10: Sarah Whitewater

well. All sections also met together in a large lecture hall to hear from a different senior professor once each week, an expert on the relevant era who typically discussed the specifics of her section material with a deeper and broader perspective. Sarah worked very hard in that class and performed very well.

At the end of the first quarter Sarah was thrilled to be invited to participate in an honors group of five students drawn from Professor Karinski's two sections for the balance of the year; reading much more extensively and meeting one evening a week in their young professor's lodgings to discuss assigned readings, typically over a single glass of wine and a different cheese each week, engaged in the most stimulating intellectual discourse of her entire life. Professor Karinski became an advocate for each new philosophy or religion as it emerged historically, challenging his students to rebut his arguments. At the end of the year they had no way of knowing his true views, but they knew very well how to articulate and defend their own.

Sarah's English composition class was almost equally fine, taught by a young woman who proudly announced midterm that her first poetry collection had been accepted for publication. Her poems had been published before,

Coyote Speaks

she said, but never in a book of their own. She was proud personally, but as an assistant professor without tenure she was also greatly encouraged by the critical acceptance of her work in the national arena in which every professor must compete to achieve tenure at a place like Stanford.

The academic side of life for a freshman anywhere is only part of the adventure. Sarah's social life was also a new experience for her, living in a women's wing of a coed residence hall among independent young people who all seemed to be worldlier than she was. Young women away from home got very close very fast and spoke openly about matters that had always been private for Sarah. The girls on her floor couldn't believe that she had never let a boy into her pants. She got the impression, surely not true, that she was the only virgin in the entire residence hall.

The "big sister" resident assistant (RA) on Sarah's floor was a great gal named Susie Hamoc, a name that prompted endless puns. As a senior Susie understood the dangers her young charges had to navigate, and she cautioned her girls with each approaching weekend about the need to stay in pairs and stay sober.

When Sarah and her roommate Sandy were approached one evening in the student union by two handsome seniors, they didn't object when the boys joined them at

Chapter 10: Sarah Whitewater

the table. As they all got acquainted the boys said they were football players (actually they were no longer with the team) and in the same fraternity, where a closed party was planned for later that night. They promised to protect the freshmen girls from the fraternity mob, and the girls were persuaded to join them at the party. Sandy and Sarah vowed between them to stick together and stay sober. The girls paired naturally with the two men, Sandy in the front seat of a sporty BMW with Jason, the dark-haired, dark-eyed boy, and Sarah in the back seat with Kris, a tall, blue-eyed blond with Nordic features.

Sandy and Sarah both expressed concern when the BMW passed through fraternity row and left campus, headed for the foothills. Kris laughingly told them the story of their off-campus housing in a splendid private home made available to them by a dedicated alumnus who objected when Stanford arbitrarily suspended the fraternity for three years and closed their campus house due to perceived hazing violations. Because the new house was five miles from campus certain alcohol restrictions did not apply. The brothers preferred their new freedoms so much that they sold their campus house to the university to become an International House and made their off-campus digs permanent. When the BMW arrived at

183

Coyote Speaks

the house, set back from the road on a half-acre lot, the girls understood the off-campus advantages.

When they passed through the security table at the fraternity house they entered a world that was utterly new to Sarah, music blasting at a level that made conversation impossible, young people dancing wildly, bodies bumping into bodies, many dancers with drinks in their hands, mugs of beer stamped with their fraternity emblem or plastic cups splashing with a red punch that was clearly not non-alcoholic. Sandy and Jason were immediately engulfed by dancers they eagerly joined, Sandy soon holding a glass of punch and Jason a beer as they danced.

Sarah had always felt awkward as a dancer; she knew that she didn't have the big boobs or the curvaceous hips she saw on the dance floor (or in the showers in the gym), but she knew that her flat belly and firm abs were the envy of every coed, so she quickly joined those girls who exposed their midriffs by tucking shirts and blouses up into their bras. The red punch gave her courage, and soon Sarah was moving pretty well and feeling pretty good.

Kris stayed by Sarah's side, as he had promised, holding her close as they danced, kissing her gently, protecting her from rowdy guys and keeping her on her feet, filling her glass continuously. Late in the evening (early in the

Chapter 10: Sarah Whitewater

morning) Sarah stumbled badly and realized that she was losing control. She told Kris that it was time for her to find Sandy and go home.

"'Sandy and Jason are downstairs," he said. "I'll take you there."

Sarah hesitated at the top of the stairs, but she trusted Kris and needed to find Sandy, so she stumbled down the stairs, needing help from Kris to stay on her feet.

The downstairs hall was dimly lit, with doors closed all along its length. Sarah and Kris entered the first door and called for Sandy, discovering an empty room with six bunk beds and a single lamp illuminating a queen-sized mattress on the floor.

Sarah again hesitated, balking a bit, but Kris took her in his arms with a full-bodied kiss, unlike those they had shared while dancing. She melted and offered no resistance when he lifted her bodily and carried her to the mattress.

Kris and Sarah lay together kissing with a greater passion than she had ever experienced, and she made no objection when he deftly unhooked her bra and pressed his mouth to her breast. Sarah had never felt so wanted by anyone, and that felt good. Her mind was fogged by the vodka in the punch, but she knew what was happening. Sarah gasped when Kris moved his hand into her panties,

Coyote Speaks

not realizing that her jeans had been unsnapped and unzipped, but she didn't scream for help. She was afraid he would do with his hand what she had done on rare occasion to herself, and when he did this Sarah groaned, which he interpreted as encouragement to move his mouth where his hand had been, her jeans and panties removed entirely. When he entered her she cried, but not with fear or anger. When he ejaculated and left her body Sarah was relieved and maybe ashamed, but she wasn't angry until she heard him say in a loud voice to his brothers then suddenly encircling them, "Okay, pledges, I got her hot for you. Show me what you can do."

Sarah may have been "dead drunk," as they say, but she was far from dead. She was having a hard time moving her limbs, but she heard every word as these callow young men (boys, really) cheered and jeered each other as they stripped naked to attack her exposed body. She struggled to lift her head and shoulders, trying to hit the skinny red-headed boy who was prying her bruised legs apart. Another boy, who smelled like vomit, grabbed her wrists from behind, so she could only twist her hips as her attacker bore down on her, trying to enter her but losing control, coming all over Sarah's belly without entering her body. The cheers turned to roars of laughter and the

Chapter 10: Sarah Whitewater

skinny boy was dragged off his victim by a big, fat man who quickly took his place, his great weight crushing Sarah's exhausted body into the mattress, his forceful entry unchallenged, her sobs swallowed by his pounding, grunting noises until she lost conscious awareness of her surroundings. Sarah never knew who followed the fat man or how many.

She woke up at dawn curled up in fetal position, covered by a thin blanket stained with blood and semen; her bra, blouse, panties and jeans strewn about near the mattress. Sarah gathered up her clothes, put them on as best she could, and snuck up the stairs and out the door, listening to laughter from the house balcony as she took what they called "the walk of shame." Sarah forced her stumbling walk into a painful jog until she rounded the corner, out of their sight, and then fell to her knees, her head buried in her hands. She was five miles from campus, five miles from her room in the dorm.

Sarah was startled by the sudden realization that a lemon-yellow VW beetle was stopped beside her with a blond, curly-headed boy, who looked maybe sixteen, standing by its wide-open passenger door, waving her in. She joined him warily but wearily, seeing no alternative. They drove without exchanging a word for several miles,

Coyote Speaks

but as they approached campus he turned to Sarah with these words: "I was a pledge at that fraternity until last night, when our pledge-master, Kris, tried to make you a part of our initiation rites. I was sickened by what they did to you, and I threw my pledge pin to the floor rather than take part. My father and my grandfather were both members of this fraternity at Ole' Miss, so they accepted me here as a legacy, but I don't belong here. I'm not one of those guys who hurt you last night. I'm sorry I couldn't make them stop."

When this young man helped Sarah out of his car at her dorm, she looked him in the eye and said "Thanks." He needed that word from her as much as she needed the ride from him.

When Sarah entered her dorm by the side door she went directly up the stairs to her fifth-floor room, found a sweat suit, and headed for the showers. She scrubbed and scrubbed, inside and out, crying quietly and alone, then crawled into bed and slept all day Sunday, the sleep of the dead. She vaguely remembered being pulled from her stupor by Susie, their ever-vigilant RA, wordlessly handing her a pill and a glass of water, waiting until she had gratefully swallowed the 'morning after' pill and then quietly withdrawing, leaving Sarah to return to oblivion

Chapter 10: Sarah Whitewater

for the rest of the day and night. On Monday morning Sarah went to class as always, rejecting Susie's efforts to get her to open up with her about her obvious trauma.

Why didn't Sarah go straight to the police with evidence of rape when she left that fraternity house? She was afraid of her parents' reaction. Sarah was afraid they would blame her for bringing this upon herself and pull her in disgrace out of her already beloved Stanford simply by denying her the partial tuition that they had been grudgingly paying. Sarah made a selfish mistake, which she didn't fully appreciate until six months later when the same fraternity was charged with a gang rape of a local high school girl; a youngster who had more courage than Sarah, a girl who would not have been raped if Sarah had blown the whistle. Three fraternity brothers went to jail, the alumnus landlord got hit by a major lawsuit, Stanford banned the fraternity, and the parent national fraternity pulled their charter. Sarah knew that she should have made this happen herself and spared this young girl the grief.

Sarah suffered every day of her life for her failure to demand justice and gain closure on her first, sad experience with sex, which she had not permitted herself to try again, even five years later. Sarah had known men she tried to love, but fear always crowded out desire. She could not cross with them this dangerous threshold. Sarah was afraid that sex in love might never be possible for her.

The trauma of her rape Sarah shared with no one, not with family, not with friends (although Sandy and the other girls knew without words from her). Sarah harbored a dark and painful secret that poisoned her relationships with men. She knew in her heart that she was capable of killing Kris, the man whose deceit ended in her rape, and she felt that she would feel the great relief that comes with revenge if she had that opportunity.

Ever since that devastating experience at the beginning of her freshman year Sarah relished the singular moment of triumph she felt when she next met Kris on campus. Sarah would not have survived at Stanford without this redeeming moment, not as good perhaps as a killing but good enough at the time to keep her from emotional collapse.

Just a few days after the fraternity house rape, Sarah and Sandy saw Kris and Jason walking toward them on the campus quad with several other guys and girls, all laughing as Kris entertained his fans, all looking at Sarah as he said in a loud voice, "There she is now. Did you get enough?"

Sarah stepped in close to Kris and slapped his face hard. He laughed at her and his circle of admirers laughed with him.

Chapter 10: Sarah Whitewater

Sarah's big brother Jack, a wrestler, often told her how to handle a man who was giving her trouble. She heard Jack's voice and did what he told her to do. Sarah can describe the scene as if unfolding in slow motion, executed perfectly as though rehearsed: She kicked Kris in the crotch with her right foot, the hard bridge of her instep catching him between the legs as a punter strikes a football; kicking with vertical power at just the right angle, her left foot briefly leaving the ground from the momentum of her leap forward but quickly rebounding as she brought her left knee high, smashing him in the face as he reflexively doubled over from the blow to his crotch; hearing the sickeningly loud "crack" as his broken nose gushed blood and he dropped to the ground groaning, lying there on his side, his knees drawn up near his chin, both hands cupped over his broken nose, blood running between his fingers. As his friends abandoned him, stepping quickly back from his pitiful body, Sarah stepped forward, pushed his hunched-over shoulder with her foot to make him face her as she glared at him, finally leaving him with these cold words: "Stop whining. If you ever mess with me again I will kill you."

Sarah never saw Kris again. According to the network of gleeful RAs, he dropped out of school, whether from injury or from embarrassment she didn't much care.

That evening Sandy dragged Sarah into the big room assigned to Susie Hamoc, their RA, where waiting for them were all the girls on their floor, an illicit bottle of champagne, and a huge sign in bold letters that read "SARAH WINS!" Indeed that night she did feel less like a victim and more like a victor in the war of the sexes. Sarah kept that feeling alive for four years at Stanford, and the memories remained with her for a lifetime.

The trauma of the gang rape haunted Sarah, raising all the self-doubts that had been with her since childhood. Why had she fallen so easily into the trap at the fraternity house? Why was she unable to report the crime or even tell her parents? Why did she feel so inadequate, despite all her successes? She talked confidentially to a counselor at Stanford late in her freshman year, a wise woman who helped her ask the right questions, but she could not help with the answers. Sarah felt that something was wrong with her as she entered adulthood, that something was missing in her life.

Sarah ran track as a miler in high school, moved into cross country running in college, and ran a marathon in

Chapter 10: Sarah Whitewater

the year after she graduated. When her girlfriends were gossiping about the latest trends in fashion magazines, Sarah was buried in *RUNNERS Journal,* imagining herself someday in a featured story. Sarah was never fast enough to win big races or to get that kind of attention, but she was good enough to make the teams in high school and college and strong enough to finish the one marathon she entered. She was never really running to win (although that was the stated goal); she was running because it made her feel good about herself.

Sarah knew vaguely that she was running away from something. She could not complain about abuse at home, but she was an unhappy child in what others surely saw as a perfectly fine family; perhaps because she never believed that she could live up to the expectations of her parents. They were both high achievers in technical disciplines, as was her big brother Jack, and all three were fiercely competitive in every arena: academically, athletically, and professionally. Sarah felt that she fell short of their expectations in all three ways, and even when she showed signs of aptitude and achievement, for example in singing folk songs with her guitar or writing poetry, those activities were dismissed in her family as frivolous.

Coyote Speaks

All through elementary school and even into junior high she was the tallest kid in class, taller even than the tallest boy, reaching 5'9" in the ninth grade and then growing no taller, very slowly building body mass as her skinny body matured. Not surprisingly, she was an awkward child, always uncomfortable with her rapidly growing body and hopeless in games requiring athleticism. All Sarah could do was run, so running was what she did.

Not only was Sarah unhappy to be so tall and clumsy, she was also unhappy about her appearance; about the wavy black hair that refused to bend into any of the current styles she was striving for; about her eyes squeezed between cheekbone and eyebrow; about everything that made her different from the popular girls in her class; and about being socially clumsy as well as physically clumsy. So Sarah ran. Maybe she was running away, running away from something.

Those features of her Indian heritage that made her feel uncomfortably different as an adolescent made her proud as a young adult. When she was at Stanford she wore her hair long and strong, and she seized every opportunity to join the girls in a ride over the hill to lie in the sun on the beautiful beaches of Santa Cruz, trying to darken her

Chapter 10: Sarah Whitewater

skin, which was too pale for an Indian girl. Sarah gradually overcame the fears of her father.

Abel Whitewater, Sarah's father, was raised by his red-headed Irish mother, a good-hearted woman born as Annie O'Rourke, a woman whose youthful vivacity was gone by the time Sarah's father defined his memories of her. Abel rarely saw his wandering Cherokee father, Adam Whitewater, whose drinking kept him in a world of uncertainty until his early death, leaving Sarah's father Abel with broken promises and dark thoughts despite his mother's best efforts to assure her son of the virtues of the man she married.

It was impossible for Sarah's father to accept the vision of his parents' youth spun by his mother: Adam as a brilliant student leader and the All-Conference running back on the football team in her high school; a handsome Indian buck who was a magnet for all the worshipful girls, including cheerleader Annie O'Rourke, who wanted him for her own. When they graduated together from high school in 1942 they were both eighteen, at a time of life when Annie was looking forward to creating a family, and Adam was torn between his aspirations for college and the excitement of going to war to defend his

Coyote Speaks

country. An American Indian boy in 1942, even one who had Adam's diverse talents and record of achievement, faced major obstacles if he aspired to college, as Adam soon realized. His uncertainties were resolved when they discovered that Annie was pregnant. They married immediately (over her father's objections) and Adam joined the Army, promising to send her his paycheck every month and return from battle to raise a family. As Abel's mother told the story, what followed is only vaguely portrayed.

As difficult as this may be for subsequent generations to understand, every eighteen-year-old man-boy in America wanted to go fight for his country in 1942, to defeat the aggressors led by Hitler, Mussolini, and Tojo. When Adam volunteered to fight, however, the US Army was still quite segregated racially, and such man-boys as Adam were relegated to kitchen duty or latrine duty, not permitted to face death on the front lines, not permitted to prove their courage and demonstrate their worthiness in battle. For Adam Whitewater this was a humiliating experience, ultimately debilitating. With other members of the kitchen crews he submerged his shame in every available source of alcohol, and his letters home (with his paychecks) stopped coming to Annie's door. When he

Chapter 10: Sarah Whitewater

was released by the Army in 1946 he was a broken man. That's the only father his son ever knew.

Sarah's own father despised his Indian heritage in consequence, and he did everything possible to overcome what he saw as the stigma of being a "breed" or "half-breed," as these derogatory labels were often used in that time and place, proving himself again and again in every arena. He considered changing his name to "Abel White," dropping the two syllables that identified him as an Indian, but hesitated too long, realizing that changing his name would erase his hard-earned reputation and sacrifice the value of his past achievements. He kept his straight black hair cut very short, military style, and stayed out of the sun, but he had the Indian look, especially around the eyes. This he could not change.

Abel Whitewater became a good middleweight boxer at Oklahoma State University, but he was admitted to the university on an academic scholarship; studying petroleum engineering through the master's degree before working for three years in the Oklahoma oil industry; starting in the oil fields and rapidly progressing into the ranks of junior executives. Always testing himself, he entered the doctoral program at his alma mater, succeeding at such a high level that he was invited upon completing his PhD to join the faculty, where his research attracted not only oil industry support but federal contracts. As his reputation grew he prospered financially as well, engaged as a technical consultant in the United States and abroad. Abel Whitewater discovered that science and technology have this in common with athletics: Performance is recognized and rewarded with little consideration of race.

Sarah's mother, Amanda, graduated in chemical engineering from the University of Iowa and accepted a graduate fellowship in petroleum engineering at Oklahoma State University, where she was dazzled in her first class by a dynamic young professor named Abel Whitewater. She wrote her master's thesis under his attentive supervision and enrolled in the PhD program to pursue an academic career as he had. After passing her doctoral qualifying exams she began her research as part of his research team. Their relationship deepened in ways unacceptable in academia, which has strict rules against romance (not to mention sex) between professors and their students. Amanda's pregnancy brought her academic aspirations to an abrupt halt. They married immediately and stayed married despite her undying frustrations with her thwarted career. She gradually came to understand that she was just as bright as her husband, but she was forever denied

Chapter 10: Sarah Whitewater

his opportunities. (At 5'8" she was just as tall, too, even in the flat heels she insisted on wearing.)

One year after her son Jack was born she accepted a job in the research lab of a local oil company in Stillwater, trying to use her talents and develop professionally in that constrained environment. When Jack was four she became unexpectedly pregnant with Sarah, further deferring her technical career until her daughter was one year old; then jumping back into the lab again, burying her ambitions in her work.

Jack and Sarah were raised in a family environment centered in the scientific and engineering work of their parents. This seemed to be a healthy situation for Jack, whose aptitudes and proclivities matched those of his parents. It didn't work so well for Sarah.

Jack was a good student in chemistry at Oklahoma State University, despite the enormous commitment he made to his athletic endeavors. But it was only after he exhausted his NCAA eligibility as a wrestler that he decided to bear down academically and try to make it into medical school with a fifth year of undergraduate study. He earned all As in that fifth year while also volunteering at the community hospital, gaining admission to the MD program at the University of Oklahoma in Oklahoma City.

Coyote Speaks

Jack was down deep an Oklahoma boy, but he qualified for an internship at Columbia Presbyterian Hospital in New York and accepted the adventure, fully expecting to return to Stillwater to practice medicine.

In the Columbia University environment Jack discovered within himself a compelling curiosity about medical science that had remained buried beneath the workload in Oklahoma. He eagerly plunged into research at every opportunity and concluded his internship with a determination to deepen his learning by pursuing a PhD in neurosciences at Columbia. Jack had shown special aptitude in his psychiatry rotation and was welcomed as a member of a research team by a professor who had herself gone the MD/PhD route. By the time Jack had finished both degrees he was committed for life to an academic career, which for him played out in New York City, first uptown at Columbia and then across town at Cornell.

Jack's parents were not happy about his move to New York City, but they were intensely proud of his success in fields they saw as akin to their own (although Jack would quietly differ). Sarah was proud of Jack, too, and she loved him beyond all measure, but his achievements made her deficiencies even more apparent.

Chapter 10: Sarah Whitewater

So Sarah ran. As her races grew longer and her training more demanding, she found that she could quiet her internal personal anxieties by immersing herself in a mind-numbing run. After her years of competitive running in high school and college were over, she found that she missed the training so badly that she committed to run a marathon and welcomed the required months of hard distance training, building up to twenty-six miles.

Sarah was told by friendly cynics that she was admitted to Stanford because an Indian cross country runner from Oklahoma with excellent high school grades added highly valued diversity to the freshman class. Her parents and her brother were scornful of the concept of affirmative action and they ridiculed Sarah for using her Indian grandfather to gain admission to Stanford. Whatever her personal circumstances, Sarah came to believe that the diversity carefully cultivated by Stanford added enormously to the value of the education available to Stanford students, who learned so much from each other because of the different perspectives each brought to the experience.

When she entered the PhD program in American Indian Studies at the University of Arizona, Sarah's family showed little respect for the undergraduate record at Stanford that got her accepted to that demanding program. They saw the extension of her studies into graduate school as another escape from reality. So she buried herself in her work, which for Sarah was another way of running.

Sarah's singular success in physically punishing Kris for his role in her rape derived from her brother's counsel as an experienced wrestler. She knew that wrestling was a tough sport, both physically and mentally, because her big brother Jack was a damned good intercollegiate wrestler and she had lived with him through both the triumphs and the trauma of this uniquely demanding and uniquely rewarding sport. Sarah attended hundreds of Jack's matches over the years, and she remembered key moments with crystal clarity.

Jack won his first Oklahoma state wrestling championship at age eight, competing, of course, with kids in his age group and weight class. In the state of Oklahoma, youth wrestling is highly competitive, so Jack benefited from excellent coaching and stiff competition for eight years even before he entered his freshman year at Stillwater High at age fourteen. He was a four-time Oklahoma State

Chapter 10: Sarah Whitewater

High School Wrestling Champion, recruited by every serious college wrestling coach in America. He chose to stay at home in Stillwater at Oklahoma State University, despite the fact that his father was on the faculty there. The National Wrestling Hall of Fame is in Stillwater, and Jack's stated goal was to win multiple NCAA wrestling gold medals and be elected to the National Wrestling Hall of Fame in his hometown.

In his freshman year at Oklahoma State University Jack lost his first match at Iowa to a more seasoned senior, who had a roaring crowd at his back, but Jack won every subsequent match that season, including the NCAA Championship. He had a fantastic start on his stated goal.

But Jack Whitewater was not the only wrestler in his weight class with such aspirations. Zack Miller at the University of Wyoming came into college a year later with the same goals and equally realistic expectations. Zack was introduced to wrestling as a boy in California and then wrestled in Wyoming high schools and the University there, all less competitive wrestling environments than Oklahoma, so he didn't have Jack's record of singular achievement at the highest levels. He received very little national recognition for remaining undefeated throughout four years at Laramie High School, where

Coyote Speaks

his father was the head wrestling coach, because he didn't face the level of competition he would have found in Midwestern or even Eastern high schools. But Zack Miller beat Jack Whitewater in the NCAA Finals for two successive years and just about broke Sarah's brother's heart. Jack was a very aggressive attack wrestler who dominated every other opponent he faced for those two years, but he couldn't seem to beat Zack Miller, a truly brilliant counter-wrestler with incredibly quick reflexes that enabled him to deflect every move initiated by Jack and turn his aggression against him. When they found themselves in an undisciplined scramble, Zack came out on top every time. Sarah had never seen a wrestler with more natural gifts for the sport.

Sarah's brother Jack entered his senior year at Oklahoma with one goal: Beat Zack Miller for the gold. Offseason conditioning put Jack in the best shape of his life entering wrestling season, and he won every match before the NCAA Championships, so he entered the biggest tournament of his life with high expectations and a second seed to his nemesis, Zack Miller.

Jack pinned every opponent on his way to the semifinals, where he met a very strong wrestler from Iowa whom he had beaten two times previously, a man who knew Jack's

Chapter 10: Sarah Whitewater

moves and defended against him very well. The first period was scoreless, and the Iowa man escaped for one point in the second period, so Jack entered the final period under great pressure. Sarah felt like she was out there with him on the mat, struggling for advantage. To her great relief, Jack reversed his opponent midway through the period for a two-to-one lead and dominated in the top position, securely in control with the exhausted Iowa wrestler flat on his belly, Jack riding him hard, only eight seconds to go. Watching from the stands, her heart exploding, Sarah began to breathe again, thinking that the match was essentially over. The referee, to the surprise of the assembly, decided to intervene, calling Jack for stalling because his hard ride on top, however vigorous, showed no evidence of a continuous effort to turn his opponent for a pin, as the rules require. The stall call created no points but it put the two wrestlers back in starting position on their knees with Jack on top, and in the remaining eight seconds the Iowa wrestler reversed her brother for two points and won the match.

This was a crushing disappointment for Jack, who might understandably have left the mat either furious with the official or sobbing at the denial of his shot at Zack Miller in the finals. Instead Jack left the mat with these words for his coach: "Now I've gotta get ready to win for third."

Coyote Speaks

And who would Jack face in the consolation match for third? Zack Miller, who got caught in a quick pin and lost his own semifinal match, had to absorb the shock and get ready mentally to battle Jack Whitewater for the bronze medal.

The winner of the last Miller–Whitewater match was the wrestler with the greatest mental toughness and emotional resilience: Jack Whitewater.

In four years Jack won four medals in the NCAA Championship Tournament: gold, silver, silver, and bronze. Jack's NCAA bronze medal, for third place, was the most significant achievement in his sixteen years of wrestling because it demonstrated that he had qualities more important in life's adventures than any physical capabilities. Jack's subsequent success in life owes more to his mental strength than to his physical skills. Wrestling is a tough sport, and Jack Whitewater was a tough guy, both physically and mentally, but the discipline of his mind turned out to be more important than the discipline of his body.

Sarah admired her brother deeply, and she loved him with all her heart, but she envied him the successes that earned the total approval of their parents, who seemed always to dismiss Sarah's own accomplishments. Maybe that was what had been gnawing at her all these years.

Chapter 10: Sarah Whitewater

When Sarah was accepted into the PhD program in American Indian Studies at the University of Arizona, she began to see herself in a new light, perhaps someday as a distinguished professor herself; an academic who could find refuge in her books, committing to total immersion in scholarly research and teaching, drowning out all her anxieties about herself.

At Arizona she was proud to be accepted in her second year into the research group surrounding Professor Alexander Dumont, whom she saw as a rising star in the field of American Indian Studies, among the most prominent ethnographers of the native peoples of the Americas. Professor Dumont was still a young scholar and, from her perspective, a man of real intellect and magnetic personality. She was determined to become his protégé, forging a brilliant academic career of her own.

Sarah performed well in her coursework and soon found herself grappling with her dissertation topic. Under the direction of Professor Dumont she outlined a dissertation to be called "Reservation Indian Assimilation," which was to identify trends in reservation populations over the past half-century, most importantly documenting the movement of individual Indians away from or back to their reservations. This was a much more difficult task

207

Coyote Speaks

than simply accounting for changes in tribal rosters, which were established by the differently defined and differently enforced rules of membership in the multitude of tribes. Her job was to determine the degree to which Native Americans had migrated successfully from their reservations into the general population; paying special attention to individuals who had been born on reservations, left them for a time, then returned to live out their lives where they were born. She was discovering that for many of the older reservation Indians she interviewed, every attempt at assimilation into the larger society had encountered obstacles or experiences that made reservation life preferable. Of course, these were the individuals who had not been assimilated into the general American population; those who had successfully transitioned would be difficult to find for interviews, so every such opportunity would be most precious. The necessary data would be difficult to obtain from many tribes, but she was to focus initially on selected tribes in Arizona and California, two states with very different reservation histories.

As Sarah plunged into her academic research, she managed to bury the traumatic memories of her rape so deeply in her subconscious mind that they very rarely surfaced to disturb her. But without her awareness she

Chapter 10: Sarah Whitewater

allowed these buried thoughts to shape her relationships with men.

She had on rare occasions found men attractive, but only from a distance. However, she had to confess to herself a powerful attraction, not just an intellectual admiration but a physical attraction, to the man she must address as Professor Dumont. She knew him to be a single man with an active social life in which she, quite properly, was not included. When Sarah and Professor Dumont traveled to Philadelphia to deliver a paper together at Penn and he invited her for a celebratory drink in the hotel bar, she was afraid to cross the line and nervously declined the offer. He had countered with a proposal to have a cappuccino at Starbucks, which she could hardly reject. Of course she didn't even hint at the unresolved trauma of her rape. But in the middle of a stimulating conversation about what Sarah could look forward to in her future life as a professor, she did burst in to tell him very directly the story of her mother's pregnancy by her father, her mother's doctoral dissertation supervisor, shattering that woman's aspirations for a PhD and an academic career. It hurt Sarah to drive Professor Dumont away so rudely, but her professor got the message and their conversation turned to strictly academic matters.

Coyote Speaks

Professor Dumont had published seminal studies that dealt comprehensively with the histories and cultures of very large and diverse populations, migrating over space and time, relying substantially on archeological evidence. He told Sarah that he had very little experience in dealing with contemporary Native Americans, especially people in tribes now settled west of the Mississippi. His Algonquin/French-Canadian ethnicity differed so dramatically from the Indians of the American Southwest that he saw people like Kit Coyote as more different from his own people than Koreans are from Japanese, and he recognized that different Indian tribes had different challenges in assimilation. He welcomed Sarah's research topic, which extended the reach of his interest in native migrations beyond archeological and historical evidence into modern times. She knew he was seriously interested in her dissertation.

Sarah knew this about the interests of her mentor professionally and was proud to share with him the emerging conclusions of her research, but she could not determine whether or not he was interested in her personally. Was he asking about her personal aspirations because he cared about Sarah in human terms, or was he equally kind and thoughtfully interested in all of his students? When he told Sarah that he was fascinated by what he called her

Chapter 10: Sarah Whitewater

"Oklahoma eyes," narrowed by the rise of her cheekbones, was he being personal or merely expressing a professional interest in Native American anatomy? Sarah wondered: *Is it possible that he is interested in me as a woman? Do I hope this is true? Or am I afraid this might be true?*

CHAPTER 11

Coming Together

In the move from Stanford to her tiny apartment near
the University of Arizona, Sarah was determined to leave
behind the detritus of her old life as an undergraduate,
but she found herself struggling with the baggage she
was determined to discard. She cast aside back issues of
RUNNERS Journal one by one, pausing to scan familiar
stories. In this way she rediscovered a feature story by
Andrea Parker about an Indian boy who had become a
hero after winning the AAU National Championship
in 1960, a boy from Tucson named Kit Coyote with an
uncertain past and a promising future. She realized that
the statistics of her dissertation were built on stories of
people like Kit Coyote, individual human beings whose
humanity could easily be lost in her statistical analyses.

Coyote Speaks

Kit was a reminder to her that research in sociology should have a human face, that her dissertation should be more than just an analysis of numbers and their averages. Sarah kept that issue of *RUNNERS* to remind her of her responsibility to humanize her research.

Sarah did wonder about Kit and wished she knew his personal story. She tracked down the expanded version of Kit's history in the book of such stories published by Andrea and her editor, but was frustrated to find that it was unclear as to Kit's origins. Was Kit Coyote born on a reservation, and if so where? And where was he now? Did he realize his promise and succeed in the white man's world, or did he fall back to the place of his birth? Sarah didn't know the answers, but she didn't forget the questions.

As the months of diligent labor over tribal statistics began to wear on her, Sarah was increasingly burdened by her fear that her dissertation would be lacking in humanity, with numbers dominating the stories she wanted to tell, stories that she knew were at the heart of the statistics that she was recording for posterity. She understood clearly that a PhD dissertation had to be substantive, with newly emerging facts constituting the scholarship of discovery that justified the award of her degree. But she felt the need to explore some of the personal stories that illustrated

Chapter 11: Coming Together

the data she had accumulated to identify the movement of Native Americans from the reservations of their birth, and often back again.

She had, of course, spoken to many of the tribal leaders as she gathered information about their people and had interviewed a good many of the individuals on the reservations who had moved back home after living off-reservation for a time. But she had less success in finding successfully assimilated reservation Indians to interview. She searched her memory for more such stories she might pursue, if only to give her the satisfaction of understanding, in a more balanced way, the human implications of her population statistics. In this search process she returned to the article she had read some time earlier about the Indian boy from Tucson. She read the story in *RUNNERS* again. She retraced the expanded version in the book written by Andrea Parker and her editor. Kit Coyote's childhood experience as a distance runner captured Sarah's interest, and she was determined to learn more. The available record indicated that he was well on his way to significant achievement in the white man's world, but Sarah could discover neither the beginning nor the ending of Coyote's personal story.

The *RUNNERS* article and the book that followed explored a question that had always been important to

Coyote Speaks

Sarah: Why do runners run? Sarah knew that her own passion for running was not driven by any special talent she had for the sport; although with hard training she was good enough to compete on the track team in high school and the cross country team at Stanford. She knew that she had a deeper motivation than the thrill of winning races, although on rare occasion she experienced this singular reward. She knew that she derived a deep kind of satisfaction from simply running, even in endless and painful practice sessions and in hard cross country races in which she had no hope of winning. She knew all this about herself, but she had always wondered if other runners were also driven by an inner hunger that could be sated only with punishing runs. The book derived from the *RUNNERS* article was asking the same questions. In particular, the story of Kit Coyote illustrated the phenomenon of the driven runner, the runner who seems to run not just to win but to exorcise his inner demons. Sarah wondered what made Kit Coyote run.

Kit went to high school in Tucson, where Sarah was doing her research at the University of Arizona, so she thought she could pick up his story most easily by contacting his foster parents, whom he called Coach and Mama K, but who were readily identified as Kenali and

Chapter 11: Coming Together

Teresa Karangetti, both in their mideighties, retired, and still living in Tucson. Sarah's phone call was warmly received, and after preliminary explorations of her reasons for knowing the Kit Coyote story, she was invited to dinner at the Karangetti home.

Sarah spent many hours with Coach and Mama K, with Ken and Teresa, both at that initial dinner and in subsequent meetings, some of which Sarah recorded for posterity. She was enthralled by the Kit Coyote story as described by the Karangettis, intrigued also by what they did not know about his origins and his ultimate fate. For Coach and Mama K, Kit's story began when he alone survived his family's automobile accident at age five, and it ended when he called from California to confess his killing of Jake Durkin, leaving key questions unresolved. Sarah decided to search for answers.

Before she found time to engage seriously in the necessary research on Kit Coyote, however, Sarah was pleased to receive the invitation from Professor Dumont mentioned previously, asking her to join him as a coauthor of a research paper that he would be presenting as the keynote speaker at an academic conference at the University of Pennsylvania. He wrote the paper partially on the basis of Sarah's research, offering her the opportunity

Coyote Speaks

to suggest changes, and asked her to join him at the conference. This would be Sarah's first participation as an author in a research conference, and the conference proceedings would be her first research publication. She was very gratified as a budding academic, but also excited at the chance to travel with her professor. As she thought about the prospect of being in Philadelphia, she began to wonder, too, if she could explore new dimensions of the Coyote story by talking to Lani Beckman's cousin Amy, if she could be located.

Coyote's story, as Sarah could decipher it, left Lani's future unresolved as her parents swept her back to Jamaica, and Sarah felt that the picture was incomplete without some knowledge of Lani's fate. She couldn't afford to track her down in Jamaica, but she sensed that Lani's cousin Amy might provide an opportunity for valuable insights. They were close enough to share the secret of Lani's love affair and marriage to Kit Coyote, so she surely knew Lani intimately and had probably known her throughout Amy's life. But would she trust Sarah with the truth? Sarah hoped that Amy would accept her as Kit's emissary if she remembered Kit Coyote sympathetically.

In the twenty-first century it's not hard to locate people on the Internet, and Sarah found that Amy Longman

Chapter 11: Coming Together

Decker lived still in the Philadelphia area. Sarah wrote her a long and quite personal letter, explaining that she was chronicling the history of the man Amy once knew as Kit Coyote, asking for an interview. To Sarah's surprise, Amy responded promptly and warmly.

Sarah met Amy in her home in Conshohocken, not far from her childhood home in Bryn Mawr but in a more modest setting. Amy was a prim, white-haired little widow in her midsixties, her voice quietly modulated and almost free of the Jamaican accent of her youth. She welcomed Sarah warmly and served tea and cookies in her patio. It soon became clear that Amy wanted to talk, if only to unburden herself of old grievances. She obviously saw Lani as a victim and her father Nigel as a villain, with poor Kit as an incidental and innocent casualty of conflicts he barely recognized.

Apparently Lani was the only child of a rich, powerful man with a meek, compliant wife; a woman so grateful for his name that she overlooked his dalliances with younger women, among other transgressions. Lani was a beautiful girl with athletic grace whose modest academic gifts merely added to her father's possessive pride.

Nigel Beckman made his fortune in the import-export business without limitations on the products and services

219

Coyote Speaks

traded; an enterprise that brought him into close relationships in government and an occasional role as an appointed commissioner of one government operation or another. His equally prominent partner in some of his business activities was a somewhat older man of good family named Arthur Thompson-Hart, whose handsome son Beau was just two years older than the lovely Lani. Both Nigel and Arthur encouraged the union of Lani and Beau, who quite naturally fell together, visible as a dazzling young couple on the Kingston social scene.

Beau had a strong sense of entitlement, and possessing Lani seemed to him to be a natural extension of his legacy. She yielded to him as her future husband, accepting her role as she accepted her anticipated inheritance. She may not have been passionately in love with her Beau, but she enjoyed the attention and played her part in Beau's wild and dissolute life.

After she graduated with modest grades from a Kingston private high school for girls, her father decreed that she should follow his sister Sophia to Bryn Mawr College in the US. She embarrassed him by gaining admission only on the condition that she first enroll and succeed in a prebaccalaureate program in America; a purgatory that brought her to an expensive prep school in the Philadelphia

Chapter 11: Coming Together

suburbs, where at least she would be able to pursue her high school interest in distance running.

Her story intersects with Kit's at that Lehigh University cross country meet. What Kit never knew is the abandonment that Lani experienced when she returned to Kingston, broken and badly burned, hospital-bound for a month and then recuperating painfully at home; her erstwhile lover Beau pursuing young women as healthy and beautiful as she once was; her father disappointed in her fall from grace and her mother increasingly absorbed in the charitable activities of her social circle. The medications prescribed to ease the pain as her burns healed became most needed to manage her psychic pain. When her prescriptions were denied, she turned to other drugs provided by her massage therapist, who soon became her lover as well. Lani's world was falling apart, and in her fantasies she created a role for Kit Coyote, the man who had saved her life, the heroic role of her rescuer. Eventually she sent him a letter, won his passionate commitment when she visited her aunt's family in Bryn Mawr, and moved to the Lehigh Valley under the pretext of attending Cedar Crest College, a respectable institution for women. Her mother and father had found her behavior increasingly embarrassing, and they were relieved to see her go.

221

Coyote Speaks

Her escape from pain in marrying Kit was only temporary, not because she didn't love him but because her wounds were beyond healing. After she crashed her car with Kit beside her and was swept back home for recuperation in Kingston, her father married her off to George Harrison, a suitor hungry for the Beckman family wealth but situated in Barbados. Lani was soon pregnant with his baby (she named him Christopher and called him "Kit"), back in touch with her American cousins and determined to rebuild her life, but tragedy struck her again.

Lani found it difficult to reconcile her drug dependency with her responsibilities as a new mother. She had always had difficulty sleeping, relying on various medications to help her sleep soundly, and a howling infant in the crib by her bed made sleeping impossible unless she brought the child to her breast in bed with her, comforting them both. This became Lani's routine, never imagining that a somnolent mother might roll over on her baby, smothering it to death. Lani gave up her life to a drug overdose soon thereafter.

As Amy recited the sad litany of events that ended in Lani's early death she spoke in monotone, almost mechanically tolling out the tragedies of her beloved cousin's charmed but cursed life experience. Tears welled

222

Chapter 11: Coming Together

up in her eyes only as she finished her story, tears that overflowed into heart-wrenching sobs. She needed to tell Lani's story to someone, and for Amy's sake Sarah was glad to be there to hear it.

She struck closer to resonance with Sarah's own life than Amy could possibly have realized. Sarah had never met Lani, but she could feel her pain, feelings she shared with a compassionate Amy. Sarah rehearsed her own unhappiness in talking to Amy, explaining that, like Lani, she had grown up in a family dominated by a strong father whose expectations of her could never be realized. Sarah's father was not the evil man that Amy saw in Lani's father, and her mother was not the weak partner that Lani's mother seemed to be, but the effects were the same. Sarah felt like a disappointment to her family.

Amy listened to Sarah's sympathetic words, paid her own emotional tribute to Lani, and then paused, clearing her throat. Sarah could see that she had more to say.

"I'm embarrassed but somehow gratified to be able to tell you that some years after Lani's passing, her father, Nigel, died in prison, died violently. He had for decades enjoyed close relationships in the power structure that governed Jamaica but fell out of favor when the political balance shifted. The new government arrested him for

223

Coyote Speaks

alleged involvement with drug smugglers, but ultimately he was charged and convicted not of smuggling drugs but of 'financing and facilitating the drug trade through money laundering,' drawing a lesser sentence than the family fearfully expected. It appears in retrospect that he negotiated his sentence by trading information about the kingpins in this dangerous business; a transaction that underestimated the power of the drug gangs to execute him in prison. Justice often comes full circle, doesn't it?"

Amy went on to assure Sarah that Lani's poor mother, Lucinda, had escaped her shame by coming to America to join Amy's mother Sophia in Bryn Mawr, where they enjoyed a comfortable life together for many years. They were not directly related, one being Nigel's wife and the other his sister, but perhaps in sharing his disgrace they bonded well together.

When Sarah returned from Philadelphia, she was eager to share her discoveries with Ken and Teresa Karangetti, and they talked more about Kit for hours one evening. Teresa shared clippings from the *Ajo Copper News* that she had saved from her initial inquiries about Kit's origins as a survivor of the family's disastrous car crash. They all wondered what that local weekly newspaper might have reported when Jake Durkin's murder was the talk of the town.

Chapter 11: Coming Together

When Sarah called the *Ajo Copper News* office the next day she was assured that they had always maintained complete archives, which she was welcome to explore in her search for more information about Kit Coyote. She was glad to put aside the statistical analyses of her tribal population demographics research for a day or two so she could drive to Ajo and examine the archive files.

Jake's murder made the front page of the *Ajo Copper News* with a headline that read "Local Rancher Murdered." The story that followed stunned Sarah, violating her sense of what had really happened to Jake Durkin. She copied the news story verbatim:

"Local Rancher Murdered"

"Jake Durkin, who has operated a chicken ranch outside of Ajo for many years, was brutally murdered by one of the many former foster children cared for by Jake and his wife Molly before her death about ten years ago. Paco Sanchez, who had become a notorious drug runner since he ran from the Durkin home at age fourteen, apparently returned as he had often promised to strangle his foster father and steal his life savings, which were held in a locked trunk in the garage of the Durkin home. Jake's housekeeper, Mary Smith, another former foster child in the Durkin

Coyote Speaks

home, was assaulted by Paco Sanchez and left tied up in the home after Jake's murder. She eventually escaped her bonds and walked into Ajo to report the crime."

Only three people could confirm or deny the validity of this news story, and neither Paco Sanchez nor Kit Coyote could be found. That left Mary Smith as the focus of Sarah's search for the truth. If she survived she would be about seventy-three years old, probably living not far from the home of her childhood. Sarah was determined to find her, hoping that she would share the secrets that surrounded the death of Jake Durkin.

Sarah tracked Mary down with some difficulty on the Tohono O'odham Reservation, starting with the mention of her full name in news accounts of Jake's death in the *Ajo Copper News* archives. Her new name, however, was Mary Norris, a widow with two children and six grandchildren, living comfortably in a nice house near the elementary school. Mary's long white hair was tied at the back but not braided, and she carried herself with dignity. She was still a sturdy, full-bodied woman but too firm to be called fat.

Mary seemed suspicious of Sarah's motives initially, but she warmed up when she was assured of Sarah's reasons for learning more about the man she knew as Kit Coyote; she was then eager to learn about "her Kit." Mary furrowed

Chapter 11: Coming Together

her brow and looked away from Sarah when she realized with a wave of guilt that Kit Coyote had been living as a fugitive for more than forty years.

"The Old Man needed to die," she said. "I coulda killed him myself, coulda slit his throat while he was sleepin', but then the law would track me down and I'd die, too. I thought there had to be a better way to kill him, and there was. Kit killed him for me.

"When you came to my house and asked about Jake's murder, I was afraid that Paco had sent you," she said. "I was afraid he would hurt me for telling the police that he had murdered Jake Durkin."

Sarah now understood the misleading story in the *Ajo Copper News*. She had assumed that Mary had protected herself by telling the truth, telling police who actually killed Jake, but it was Mary who had pointed to Paco.

Mary continued talking, relieved to finally share her secret with someone. "Everybody knew by then that Paco was a killer for the drug bosses, so making Jake's death Paco's doing just added to his reputation in his dirty business. When Paco was at the Durkin ranch, and even later, he kept on boasting that he would someday wring The Old Man's scrawny neck, take his little brass key, and raid his red trunk of its treasure. It was very easy for me to feed

Coyote Speaks

the natural suspicion that it was Paco who murdered Jake and raided his red trunk. The *Ajo Copper News* reported as a matter of fact that it was Paco Sanchez who broke Jake's neck, to no one's surprise. I did worry that Paco might find out about my accusation and come after me, but that fear has faded over the years. Paco must be in his midseventies now if he's still alive, so I think I'm safe." Mary took a deep breath, not accustomed to long speeches.

"Mary," Sarah said, "did you tell Kit that you would keep him out of it by blaming Paco?"

"I don't know," Mary confessed. "I tried to tell him he'd be safe if he ran, and I know I told him not to worry, but I don't think I told him my plan to blame Paco. After he was gone I had no way to reach him, and I had other things to worry about. I'm sorry if that made him suffer."

"Mary, you speak of your plan to blame Paco. When Kit killed Jake you seem to have taken charge as though you knew exactly what to do next. You seemed to be acting from a well-conceived plan. How did you know that Kit was coming before he knew it himself? Why were you so well prepared?"

"I didn't know Kit was coming, but that was my dream. I felt sure that one of the boys from the ranch would come back to kill that evil man, for revenge or for his money

Chapter 11: Coming Together

or for both. I hoped it would be Kit, my favorite among the boys after Timmy took his own life, but it could have been Diego or Paco. I knew that Kit or Diego would not hurt me and would share whatever we found in the trunk. If either had arrived at my door and managed to kill Jake, I would have blamed Paco. If Paco had arrived at my door I would have watched him kill Jake and then run for my life while he raided the red trunk."

Mary and Sarah parted with a warm hug and Sarah's assurance that she would do everything possible to find Kit and tell him her story. She didn't know how she would track Kit down after all these years, but she was determined to try.

Catty had read in the *Ajo Copper News* that Jake Durkin had been murdered in his kitchen, his neck broken by the notorious drug runner Paco Sanchez. But she knew that it had to be Kit Coyote who had killed The Old Man, not Paco. She wished she could have been there to witness the deed, wondering how little Kit Coyote could have broken the neck of a man twice his size. (Catty would still be thinking about Kit as that skinny little pipsqueak she knew at the ranch.)

Catty felt pride in her own role in firing up Kit's anger the night before he confronted Jake, leaving her in their

Coyote Speaks

rumpled bed without a word of explanation or farewell. He had many good reasons to strangle The Old Man, but she had added Snow to Kit's long list of grievances. She was pleased to share with Kit Coyote the secret of The Old Man's violent death. She would never tell anyone who killed Jake Durkin.

When Sarah came to Ajo to search for new pathways to Kit Coyote, after she found Mary and discovered the truth about Jake's killing, she made a futile attempt to find Catty, who had disappeared without a trace a decade earlier. Had she finally found the man who could take her away from her dark life, or had that life engulfed her?

As Sarah searched the archives of the *Ajo Copper News*, reading the account of Jake's murder more than once, she turned her attention to the accounts of Kit's survival of his family's automobile crash when he was just five years old. She had read these clippings at the Karangetti house, but she poured over them again, searching for some new clue to Kit's identity. Her eyes fell upon these words in the first story: "Fierce flames destroyed all evidence of the identity of the family members, except possibly for four items of jewelry." Is it possible, she wondered, for those jewelry pieces to be still somewhere in the property room of the Ajo Police Department?

Chapter 11: Coming Together

Police headquarters in Ajo was not a busy place when she dropped in there, and the sergeant at the front desk was easy to talk to. He was an old guy, probably Hispanic or Indian or both, not far from retirement, and he hoped as Sarah entered the door that she would bring him something interesting.

"Problem?" he said.

"No problem," said Sarah, "just a puzzle from the past that I hope you can help me with."

"I'm Sergeant Mendez, and I know all about the past. It's the future I'm worried about. I've been on the force here since I was a kid, trying to keep this town safe in the middle of a war zone. What do you need to know?"

"There was a terrible automobile accident just south of town on 85 in August of 1946, killing three members of an unidentified family. A five-year-old child survived the crash; he was placed as a foster child on the Durkin ranch. He never knew his family name, and that's what I'm looking for. The paper reported four pieces of jewelry as artifacts of the fire, and I'm looking for some evidence of those remnants here in your archives."

"Was that the foster kid who came back to murder old Jake Durkin? One of those drug runners, back to claim the old man's gold and his life?"

231

Coyote Speaks

"The paper said that the killer was Paco Sanchez, and that's not the boy who survived the fire. His name was Joey. They called him Kit Coyote, but he never knew his real family name."

"I'm an old man, lady, and I was born in 1946. Ain't nobody around here can remember that car crash, or half the crashes on 85 since that one. We got records fillin' the archives and lots of old stuff in the property room, but we'd be lucky to find what you're lookin' for."

"I've been through your print archives and found reference to four artifacts of the car fire that killed Kit's family, four pieces of jewelry. Now I'd like to look for that jewelry and see if there are any engravings that might identify the family name. Can you show me your property room?"

"I'd like to help you, lady, but I can't leave my post here 'til I get spelled at noon. If you want to wait a couple hours I can open up the property room for you during my lunch break, but I'll need to see an ID first and stay with you in the room. We try real hard to run a clean house with good controls."

Sarah quickly agreed and waited patiently for two hours, her hopes for some kind of discovery growing unreasonably with each passing hour. When Sergeant

232

Chapter 11: Coming Together

Mendez broke for lunch and led her to the property room, she had high expectations.

What the Ajo Police Department called a property room was unimpressive... a rather small, windowless room at the back of the building; all four walls lined with deep shelves cluttered with all kinds of stuff, with a desk and filing cabinets in the middle of the room.

Sergeant Mendez led Sarah directly to the files, which were chronological. Sarah caught her breath when she saw in the 1946 file reference to jewelry salvaged from an automobile accident, but sighed to discover that the four articles of jewelry had been transferred to Jake Durkin soon after he accepted the surviving boy as his foster child. Sarah knew she would never see that jewelry, but she read the file carefully in the hope of finding relevant descriptions of the missing artifacts. She was not disappointed.

The clerk for the property room in 1946 had recorded all inscriptions found on the jewelry, so Sarah discovered the father's name to be J. R. Hyde and the mother's name to be Maria, both critical pieces of information. Perhaps more importantly, she recognized the name of the Morongo tribe inscribed on the mother's cross. She was quite familiar with this Southern California tribe from her dissertation studies and knew they kept good historical records. Sarah

233

decided to extend her break from her scholarly studies and drive a few hours to the Morongo Reservation.

Thanks to a thriving hotel/casino and a substantial complex of outlet stores, the Morongo Reservation Sarah visited in her quest was a far cry from the impoverished cluster of aging homes that Kit knew as a child. She spent the night at the hotel and presented herself and her credentials to the chairman's office the next morning, seeking historical information about the Joseph R. Hyde family. The young woman at the reception desk was most obliging in searching the files under the name Hyde and soon confirmed that Joseph R. Hyde had lived on the reservation with his family of four (including two boys named Jimmy and Joey) until the summer of 1946. Her files had no reference to the fatal accident that had destroyed his family, so Sarah offered the information that concluded the life story of the J. R. Hyde family, noting the survival of their youngest son.

Satisfied that she had resolved the mystery of the origin of the child known to her as Joey Kit Coyote, gratified that his history matched the pattern of so many other

Chapter 11: Coming Together

reservation Indians in her study, Sarah got to her feet and expressed her thanks to the young woman for sharing the files, preparing to head back to Tucson.

"Don't you want to talk to Coyote Viejo?"

Sarah couldn't believe that she had heard correctly. "Was Coyote Viejo once known as Kit Coyote? Are you telling me that a man named Coyote lives here on the reservation now?"

"I know him as Coyote Viejo, but he should be able to answer your questions. I'll call his house and see if he'll come down to talk to you."

Sarah hesitated, realizing that Kit Coyote was now an old man, probably now known as Coyote Viejo but still thinking of himself as a fugitive, not realizing that Mary had long ago deflected police attention to Paco. Sarah asked the young woman not to call Coyote Viejo but instead to share with her any relevant information in their personnel files and then to tell her where he lives, so she could surprise him with good news.

When she reached his modest house she found him sitting on the doorstep with three small boys in the dirt at his feet, obviously enthralled with some story he was telling with great enthusiasm. Sarah watched Coyote and the boys from her car, unnoticed for several minutes, until

235

Coyote Speaks

finally he looked up and with some difficulty got to his feet and moved toward her. She jumped out of her car and met him not twenty feet from his house, apologizing for watching him unannounced as he entertained the boys. She quickly told Kit that she had good news for him and asked if they could go inside.

Although Coyote Viejo had been animated and most expressive when he was talking to the boys, his demeanor as Sarah told her story was initially impassive. As she began to ask him questions, however, he was suddenly angry.

"No," growled the grizzled old Indian, his voice surprisingly strong for a man in his condition, his square jaw then set, his teeth clenched as if to prevent Sarah from forcing him to speak.

"Why should I speak now, after all these years? I don't want to talk about the past."

"Yes," said Sarah quietly, the rhythm of her melodic voice somehow soothing to his ear, "you do want to talk about your past. I'm told that you are a great storyteller, that you talk for hours with the children here on the rez and they believe everything you say. Your tribal records tell me that you left the reservation as a boy and returned after many great adventures, so I know you have a story to tell. I know, too, that your time here is limited. I can

Chapter 11: Coming Together

record your stories for future generations so they will know what you accomplished as a young Indian in the white man's world, so they will set their own sights high."

"Why do you say my time is limited? What do you know about my cancer?" The old man was now whispering hoarsely, his visage changing, softening, his voice quavering, breaking with the word *cancer*. "They tell me that pancreatic cancer is a killer. What you say may be true: I speak now or never."

As Sarah found her voice and explained her discovery that Coyote has not been a fugitive all these years in California, she finally got through to him.

"True?" he kept saying as she explained Mary's deflection of his crime to Paco. "True?" "Can all this be true? Why didn't Mary tell me that she would protect me?"

Coyote's expression softened as he absorbed the import of Sarah's explanations; his attempt at stoicism gradually fell away, and his voice began to fade. "Why didn't she tell me? I've been living in fear for more than forty years, only gradually accepting the success of my escape from punishment. Why didn't she tell me?"

Finally Coyote came to his feet, moving with surprising agility into the adjacent small kitchen, and asked Sarah if she would like a cup of coffee, explaining that they

237

Coyote Speaks

would both need a little coffee if she was going to listen to his story as he had lived it for seventy years. She was surprised by his sudden change in demeanor and anxious to hear his story in his own words. They settled down at the kitchen table with her digital recorder for a very long session.

She knew from tribal records that this old man they called Coyote Viejo (evidently Kit Coyote as a boy) was born and christened Joseph Charles Hyde right there on the Morongo Reservation in 1941, delivered by a tribal midwife, so that now in his seventieth year he would soon die here as well. For many of the old men Sarah had already interviewed, all the years from birth to death had played out on their reservations; gone perhaps for a few painful years of military service; complicated perhaps by brief and discouraging sojourns into neighboring cities and towns; but always returning to the only place that ever felt like home. For this Coyote, however, the world had reached beyond the reservation. Sarah knew that she must hear his story from him directly.

She found that the old man could weave words with the voice of an old Indian storyteller, but at the same time speak in correct sentences like an English teacher. He rambled on at great length without his pause or her

Chapter 11: Coming Together

interruption, using language not so very different from her own, but he growled where Sarah would sing. She wondered how she could capture this difference on the printed page. She wouldn't be able to record the timbre of this old man's voice in her transcription, but she was determined to do her best to convey not only his thoughts but the intensity of his feelings.

As Sarah listened to Kit tell his story and gradually came to appreciate the complexities of his life experience, she was drawn into his narrative and increasingly engaged in his humanity. Listening for hours to the strange tale of Kit's lifelong struggles, she began to see herself more clearly, to realize that Coyote's triumph over seemingly overwhelming adversities spoke forcefully to her.

If young Kit Coyote could not only survive the sudden death of his entire family when he was five years old, but also endure homelessness and the exploitation in foster care that followed, then surely Sarah could overcome the modest imperfections in her childhood environment. If as a young man Kit could recover from a dangerous infatuation that put him at risk of surrendering to alcohol and other drugs and sacrificing his hard-won career as teacher and coach, then surely she should be able to cope more effectively with the trauma of gang rape without permanent

Coyote Speaks

damage to her ability to love a man. If after killing his childhood tormentor and solving the mysteries of his identity Coyote could redefine himself and for the second time earn professional credentials, then Sarah should be able to overcome her more modest problems and create for herself a healthy and fully-developed personal and professional life. If Coyote could breathe freely, surely Sarah could learn to breathe freely, too.

Sarah was ultimately so inspired by Coyote's tale of triumph over tragedy that she vowed internally to confront her own relatively modest problems; resolved to establish for herself a healthy life free from preoccupation with the singular tragedy of the fraternity rape or the nagging concerns about parental expectations. She realized, of course, that Coyote's spirit was liberated by the truth, that his ultimate redemption required the sharing of secrets. She knew that she had to share her secrets, too, if she wanted to liberate her own spirit.

Sarah knew in her heart what she had to do, but she didn't know how to do it. There was only one person in her life she could hope to understand her reaction to that rape, now almost six years ago. Her parents would be angry at her failure to report the crime immediately and skeptical about her response that her fear of their reaction was

Chapter 11: Coming Together

the reason for her silence. Big brother Jack might respond sympathetically, but he might also track Kris down and kill him even now, essentially ending Jack's life as well as his victim's. No, the only person Sarah wanted to talk to was Alex Dumont, but she feared that opening up such personal matters could jeopardize their professional relationship. The last time he tried to engage her in anything approaching a personal conversation she rudely drove him away. Now she had to find a way to talk to him about personal matters without losing his professional respect.

Sarah pushed hard to finish her dissertation ahead of schedule so she could get on with her life. In final form her PhD thesis documented the movement of Indian people to and from their reservations with very little statistical evidence of the reasons for such movement, which was often erratic. She concluded her thesis with a chapter that speculated on those reasons, using several anecdotal stories to illustrate her belief that persistent obstacles made it very difficult for American Indians to integrate successfully into the larger communities beyond their reservations. Coyote's story was the richest in meaning to Sarah, but all of these stories were revealing in a socio-historical sense, together providing her dissertation with a human dimension that added weight to her statistical analyses.

Coyote Speaks

When she submitted her first draft to Professor Dumont, he expressed his general approval after his first reading and asked Sarah to make an appointment in his office for specific suggestions for revisions. She asked him if he would meet her at her apartment, where she told him she kept voluminous files and where she claimed to be eager to try out her new cappuccino machine. Professor Dumont made a small joke about avoiding "inappropriate intimacy," but he accepted Sarah's proposal.

Sarah rushed out to buy a new cappuccino machine and cleaned her apartment, more anxious about his visit than she wanted to be.

When Professor Dumont arrived he and Sarah spent the first fifteen minutes trying to figure out her expensive, multipurpose coffee machine, laughing together about the benefits of liberal education. He asked her to call him Alex, which she was very comfortable doing.

They did spend more than an hour reviewing her dissertation draft, referring occasionally to Sarah's files, and Alex came to appreciate the depth of her admiration for Coyote's ability to overcome adversities, acknowledging that she hadn't done as well herself.

"What adversities do you need to overcome?" he asked, leaving Sarah unable to respond for a long moment. When

Chapter 11: Coming Together

she finally found the courage to answer his question, she told him everything.

Even before Alex could respond, Sarah felt a profound sense of relief; she had finally shared her dark secrets with someone she trusted. When Alex had a moment to transform his image of Sarah, stripping away his impression of her as a serious student with a frozen façade, he gave her his hand and stole her heart.

"You'll be okay," he kept saying. "Trust me to help you through this. You'll be okay. In fact, you'll be marvelous."

Alex insisted that exposing her secrets to fresh air and sunlight would ease her pain, urging Sarah to open up her heart and talk freely about her darkest memories, even to write about her most difficult experiences. She told him then that as a lonely girl at Stanford she had kept a personal journal and in it she had written a full description of her trauma and its aftermath. She offered to share her journal with him, even those passages that might prove to be embarrassing to her.

In the days and weeks that followed, Alex read her journal and made her believe his words. He even made her believe that they would have a future together as soon as she removed the obstacle created by their professional relationship, which obstacle she could overcome simply by

243

Coyote Speaks

finishing her PhD. She didn't tell him so then, but Sarah knew that she was prepared to give Alex all her love, her body as well as her heart. She knew, too, that he felt the same way.

Among the many lessons Sarah learned from Coyote was the importance in his life of his identity, his childhood name, and his Morongo tribal heritage. We all need to know who we are, she realized, and Coyote's sense of himself was incomplete without knowledge of his own name and his tribal roots. At the same time it became clear in his telling of his story that Joseph Charles Hyde is also Kit Coyote, who is not just a Morongo Indian but also a runner, a wrestler, a husband, a coach, and a teacher, perhaps most of all a teacher. These lessons applied to her, too. She had been trying to lose herself in the singular identity of a scholar of American Indian Studies with hopes of becoming a professor in this field; relying unduly upon her grandfather's status as a full-blooded Cherokee to define who she was; suppressing every other important dimension of herself as a woman, a sister, and a daughter, and perhaps someday as a lover, a wife, and mother. Sarah's life was really just beginning as Coyote's time on earth was coming to an end. Such is the cycle of nature, Sarah thought, but she didn't begin this adventure with such a noble vision.

Chapter 11: Coming Together

All of these changes in her sense of herself she owed to Coyote. The man she came to know as Joseph Coyote Hyde was finally recognized as an extraordinary human being, fully deserving of deeper and more widespread understanding than Sarah could ever hope to provide through a chapter in her doctoral dissertation. Sarah began to dream about writing the book that Coyote deserved.

Sarah forced Coyote to face reality; he realized that he had to tell his story "now or never." He wondered if telling his story might ease his pain. And he thought maybe, just maybe, he could talk about his climb to the top of the mountain of dreams in ways that would inspire young Indians to follow their own dreams, as he did so many years ago.

Coyote's lengthy soliloquy in talking to this young woman called Sarah was strangely liberating. It felt good to say things he had never said before to anyone, not even Anna, and expressing these buried thoughts made him feel better about himself. In talking about Lani, he better understood why he was so vulnerable to self-destructive behavior, when in the past his actions had seemed to be

Coyote Speaks

just stupid and irrational. When he faced the passions of his confrontation with Jake, and accepted the reality of his killing as necessary for his own survival at that moment, he could forgive himself in a way not previously possible for him.

Most critically, of course, Sarah had discovered that Mary had covered for Coyote, blaming Paco for killing Jake Durkin, so the police were never looking for Kit Coyote. All those years when he behaved like a fugitive, he was subjecting himself to unnecessary stress, allowing fear to drive his behavior. When Sarah told Coyote that Mary had concealed his involvement in Jake's death without telling him of her intentions, leaving Kit to suffer in fear for decades, he was deeply relieved and at the same time angry at Mary. Upon reflection, however, he didn't remain angry or long harbor the initial feeling of betrayal. Had he not been seeking a new identity he might never have learned his true name. He would surely not have stumbled across his Morongo heritage as he fled to Los Angeles; he would not have been fleeing at all. Kit would not have met Anna, with whom he enjoyed an intimate friendship over many years and a long and entirely agreeable marriage. He had to prove himself twice to earn the privilege of teaching and coaching in both Pennsylvania and California, but he

Chapter 11: Coming Together

actually enjoyed all those years in college and benefited enormously from his formal education. As he looked back upon a life full of joys and sorrows, Coyote had no regrets; he knew that he could die in peace whenever his time came. When he said goodbye to Sarah she knew he would be at ease for the rest of his life.

Despite the cancer spreading from his pancreas, Coyote still managed to make his way to Riverside for occasional events on the university campus, and he still enjoyed spinning tales for the children on the reservation. Life was still good.

And so it happened that Coyote was a front-row witness when a wild-eyed man with a shaved skull turned his assault rifle on three panelists on a university auditorium stage, killing the local imam and badly wounding the rabbi and the priest; all three convening to urge peaceful understanding among the Muslim, Jewish, and Christian students in the assembly. Coyote was shot dead when he stood to face the gunman, who then took his own life as well.

Coyote's life ended sooner than he expected, but it ended quickly and heroically.

Cast of Characters
(In alphabetical order)

Abel Whitewater	Sarah's father
Adam Whitewater	Abel's father, Sarah's Cherokee grandfather
Alexander Dumont	Sarah's professor at the University of Arizona
Amanda Whitewater	Sarah's mother
Amy Longman Decker	Sophia's daughter, Lani's cousin
Andrea Parker	reporter for RUNNERS Journal
Anna Czova	Banning High School librarian, Kit's second wife
Annie O'Rourke	Abel's mother, Sarah's grandmother
Arthur Thompson-Hart	Nigel's business partner, Beau's father
Aunt Sophie Longman	Lani's aunt on her father's side
Beau Thompson-Hart	Arthur's son, Lani's fiancee
Billy Sheridan	Lehigh University wrestling coach
Catty	Durkin foster child (aka Cat)

Coyote Speaks

Christopher "Kit" Harrison	Lani's infant son
Coach K	Dr. Kenali Karangetti
Coyote	book's central figure (aka Kit Coyote, Coyote Viejo, Joey Kit Coyote, Joseph Charles Hyde)
Damian O'Brian	Lehigh wrestler, Kit's roommate
David Chen	Lehigh University cross country coach
Diego Rivera	Durkin foster child
Doc Feldman	ranch veterinarian
Dominic Karangetti	Kenali & Teresa's son
Dr. Eduardo Ramirez	Ajo grade school principal, brother to Teresa Karangetti
Dr. Gutierrez	Aunt Molly's physician
Emily Chu	Anna's mother
George Harrison	Lani's husband in Barbados
Jack Whitewater	Sarah's brother
Jake Durkin	The Old Man, who ran the chicken ranch and foster home
James Jackson	Jimmy's birthfather
Jason	frat boy who paired with Sandy
Jimmy Jackson Hyde	Kit's older brother
Joseph Charles Hyde	Kit's name at birth
Joseph R. Hyde	Kit's father
Kira Karangetti	Kenali & Teresa's daughter
Kris	frat boy who paired with Sarah

Cast of Characters

Lani Beckman	Kit's first wife (aka Lani Coyote, Lani Harrison)
Lucinda Beckman	Lani's mother
Mama K	Teresa Karangetti, Coach K's wife, formerly Teresa Marshela Ramirez
Maria Hyde	Kit's mother, formerly Maria Jasmin Alto
Mary Smith	Durkin foster child (aka Mary Norris)
Miguel	Sunnnyside High School wrestler
Miss Mabel Fitzgerald	English teacher at Sunnyside High School
Miss Mildred (Billie) Hunkin	Sunnyside High School librarian
Molly Durkin (Aunt Molly)	Jake's wife
Mrs. Hawkins	motel proprietress
Natalie Longman	Sophia's daughter, Lani's cousin
Nigel Beckman	Lani's father
Paco Sanchez	Durkin foster child, later drug runner
Pastor Bob	Molly's Southern Baptist Church minister
Professor Karinski	Sarah's World Civilizations professor at Stanford University
Professor Peter Beider	Kit's English professor at Lehigh University
Queen	German Shepherd dog, Solo's mother

Coyote Speaks

Sandy	Sarah's roommate at Stanford University
Sarah Whitewater	University of Arizona grad student
Sergeant Mendez	officer at the Ajo police station
Snow	Durkin foster child
Solo	Kit Coyote's coydog, born to Queen
Susie Hamoc	resident assistant (RA) in Sarah's Stanford dorm
Tennyson "Tenny" Stark	Lehigh football player, Kit's housemate
Thomas "Jeff" Bingham	Lehigh basketball player, Kit's housemate
Timmy	Durkin foster child (aka Timoteo Blanco)
Zack Miller	Wyoming wrestler, Jack's nemesis
Zdenic Czova	Anna's father

About the Author

Peter Likins is president emeritus of the University of Arizona and former president of Lehigh University. He served earlier in his academic career as an engineering professor at UCLA, advancing to Columbia University as dean of the School of Engineering and Applied Science and then as provost of the university.

Educated as an engineer at Stanford and MIT, and engaged as a spacecraft development engineer by the Cal Tech Jet Propulsion Laboratory in 1958, the very first year of the Space Age, Likins is a Fellow of the American Institute of Aeronautics and Astronautics, and a Member of the National Academy of Engineering.

Captain of the Stanford wrestling team and silver medalist at the Pacific Coast Conference Tournament and the Far Western Championships, Likins is recognized as

Coyote Speaks

an "Outstanding American" in the National Wrestling Hall of Fame in Stillwater, Oklahoma.

Dr. Likins is the author or coauthor of several engineering textbooks and a personal memoir, *A New American Family: A Love Story*, describing the experiences of his interracial family, which includes six adopted children, black, white, and brown, all born in California in the 1960s.

Peter Likins and his wife Patricia celebrate sixty years of marriage in their Tucson, Arizona home.

CPSIA information can be obtained at www.ICGtesting.com
Printed in the USA
LVOW07s2203030316

477708LV00001B/13/P

9 780997 042344